Circumstances

a novel

by Yolanda M. Johnson

Published by
LITERARYWONDERS!
Literary Wonders!
P.O. Box 295177
Lewisville, TX 295177
http://www.literarywonders.com

This book is a work of fiction. Names, characters, places and incidents are products of the author's imagination or are used fictitiously. Any resemblance to actually events or locales or person, living or dead, is entirely coincidental.

LCCN 2005906758
ISBN   0-9770403-0-5

Printed by
Lightning Source Inc
1246 Heil Quaker Blvd
La Vergne, TN USA 37086
Email: enquiries@lightningsource.co.uk

Cover Graphics, Design, and layout by Candace K. Cotrell

First Printing October 2005

Printed in the United States of America

In Memory Of

Betty Sue Johnson.

(March 20, 1948 – July 26, 2001)

And

Larry Dale Renfroe

(January 6, 1952 – March 28, 2003)

Acknowledgements

Praises and Thanks to my Lord and Savior, for blessing me over and beyond. Thank you for blessing me with the gift of words. For without you, I am nothing.

Thanks to my children, NeCoyia Michelle Smith and Tyre Rashaad Smith, for bringing me so much joy and motivation to write this book. I love you both and am proud of you both. Always, put Christ first in all that you do, and never settle for anything less than the best.

Acknowledgements to the Burleson Family. To Sydney and Doug Adams, may you both rest with the Master. Thank you to Loving Saints Christian Fellowship. To Brenda Renfroe, thank you for everything! Duena Watkins, your blessing is on the way. Thank you to Bishop Joel David Trout and the rest of the North Park Apostolic family. To Myra Green, thanks for everything. To my Stephen Green, you need Jesus and a clue, but I love you anyhow. Stop runnin' through them women like you do underwear. It's a thin line between love and hate and you know I don't do funerals.

Special thanks to Sylvia Willis Lett, Parry 'Ebony Satin' Brown, Shelia M. Goss, Vanessa A. Johnson, Margie Gosa Shivers, James Lisbon and AMAG and Mrs. Emma of Black Images Book Bazaar.

Thanks to the following authors and literary padres for touching my life in one way, shape, form or fashion: Vincent Alexandria; with your cute self, Victor McGlothin; Mr. Victor Said Himself!, Kim Robinson; When am I going to see my better than sex cake recipe in print??? *smile*, Shelia Goss; you are a tremendous and awesome help and resource, My Three Beaus will be at the top of the best seller list, Sylvia Lett; Thank you for I Wish I Had Waited, Delores Thornton; Miss Radio, thank you lady, Gail McFarland; my editor yall!, Eric Pete; my boy, Can't Stop, Won't Stop, Believe That!, Tina McKinney. Say cheese!, "Bozz"; stop procrastinating and just do the dayum thang!, Nicole Stevenson, Harold Turley; boy if you wasn't my lil' brother, we'd tear Dallas up!, Misherald Brown; take care of my neice/nephew, Zane; thank you for reminding me what sexuality is girl! lol, now slow down and give us other black folk a chance, Tyler Perry; you are too retarded, but in special way. I felt guilty buying that first Madea bootleg.. QQ... so I went out and bought the rest *smile*, Linda Chavez; the fastest reader on the net, Lissa Woodson, Kendra Norman Bellamy, Essense; thank you for Divas, Karen Quinones Miller, Janet Sellars, Nikki Woods, Cruze, Gary Johnson; thank you for my piece in Black Men In America, Jessica Tilles, Omar Tyree; I'll tell you what I gotta say in person, Parry Brown; style, sophistication and grace, and you were unselfish and I admire you for that, Lee Hayes, Kim, Floyd,

Rowena Winfrey; when are we going out again?, Shelly Hallima; where IS my toy, I mean my gift?, Cydney Rax, Michael Everhardt, Lolita Allen, Phil Andrews, Mya B.,Tee Brown, Malik Canty, Gregory Bryant, Michael T. Owens, Nane Quartay, Heather Covington, Donna Hill, Frances Ray, Monique Bruner; my associate editor, thanks for your hard work, and John A. Wooden.

To everyone in my "online" family, WritersRX, RealSisterWriters, RAWSISTAHZ, ReadinColor, APOOO411, SistahsInSpirit, DivasofEssence, Blackexpression2005, Romance Noire, KimsCrew, 30s Talent, Shades of Romance, Group One Online, Prolific Writers, and the numerous others that are too many too name.

Also to my "2005 Anthology Project" authors, Vanessa A. Johnson, Toschia, Rowena Winfrey and Kim Robinson. We're almost done and I Love you all, even though yall worked my nerve. Can we get this done already?

To Meesha, you ain't grown lil heffa. To Kei, keep your head up, leave those lil boyz alone, get yourself together and God will send you a man. Many thanks to Bennie Patridge. Thanks for giving the baby my middle name.

A big, big thanks to T-bone Tamra Bedford and your family for your unlimited support and belief in my project. For keeping me somewhat level headed and preventing me from having to take anger management classes and going to jail. You have no idea. To Miss Sheree, Mama wait until you read the sequel, you're going to need a whole bottle of wine! To Tori, my new junior editor and reviewer, and buddy, love you much. To Tina, love you much and sometimes I wonder if you know just how blessed you are. To my softball team; Goooooooooooooo Rattlers!!

To Candace Cotrell, my graphic artist, who "did the dayum thang" on my cover. Thank you girlfriend. To Al Henry, the best darn manager a girl could have. Kudos to Andria Owens and grandbabies Cheyenne and Keyonna. Just keep doing what you do and the rest will fall into place. Hugs to Timothy Watts, U were scared huh? *smile*, to my little brother George Badgette, you can't turn a hoe into a housewife and you can't blind man into a good man if he can't see. Do you before you try to do anybody else. To Melissa, my reviewer, let go and let God. Patricia, you are truly a light.

Shout outs to Seth Nelson, Jerry Beck; ump humph umph, Jonathan and Leola Harkless. Jonathan, thank you for showing me the heart and soul of a man. Gary Alexander; words will never explain, Charlie and Elaine Michaels; kill Bailey for me.

If I've forgotten anyone, please charge my head and not my heart. You all know I'm getting old and senile. Oh Yea, Go Cowboyz!! And Go Lakers! QQn @ Gary Moore and you thought it was over didn't ya?!

<u>Leviticus 17</u>: Thou shalt not uncover the nakedness of a woman and her daughter, neither shalt thou take her son's daughter, or her daughter's daughter, to uncover her nakedness; for they are her near kinswomen: it is wickedness.

<u>Genesis 9:</u> And the LORD said unto *Cain*, Where is *Abel* thy brother? And he said, I know not: Am I my brother's keeper?

My Daughter's Keeper

Am I my daughter's keeper?
Am I to teach her the things
The things she should know
To grow into the woman she is to be?
Yes I am my daughter's keeper.

Am I my daughter's keeper?
Am I to protect her from all
That life has prepared for her
To destroy and kill her?
Yes I am my daughter's keeper.

Am I my daughter's keeper?
Am I to instill in her love and respect
For herself and others
To teach her right from wrong
Yes I am my daughter's keeper

Am I my daughter's keeper?
Am I to raise her to despise her
To envy all that she has come to be
Knowing that what she is should be me
Yes I am my daughter's keeper

Am I my daughter's keeper?
Am I to keep her from hungry hands?
Foul minds and bedroom eyes
Or do I let them devour her in the night
Am I really my daughter's keeper?

Yolanda M. Johnson ©

Violation n.

> **1. Breaking of the law; transgression breach, trespass, defiance, infringement, felony, crime, misdemeanor, non-observance.**

> ***2. Rape, molestation, sexual abuse, sexual assault, deflowering.***

> ***3. Desecration, disrespect, defiling degradation.***

> **4. Invasion of privacy, invasion of one's space, disturbance.**

Prologue

September 24, 1968

The searing heat beamed down on the family of trees in the desolate backyard. The humidity rising from the ditch out back was rancid, mosquitoes abundant. Murky brown elixir, lurking like volcanic lava behind the derelict shack gave way to southern stench. Cracking paint graced the structure, adorned by its broken windows and rickety boards. Transgressed cement, an evil sanctuary, sufficed as a foundation covered in tall, uncut grass; the devil's first formation lurking beneath.

Silence broken as the depressed heavens peeked through the emerald forest. Innocence of life skipping along, chasing butterflies. Innocence startled.

"Babra' Jean, get yo' tail in hea' and clean dis' house." Memah stood short and petite yelling from the screen door; hanging onto its last hinge. Barbara Jean scurried up the mangled steps into the kitchen. The aroma of salt pork danced a jig.

"When I get back, I want dem clothes hangin' out on dat line. I want dis kichen' flo' scrubbed an' I want dat wall dere in da bafroom washed."

"Yes Ma'am," Barbara Jean answered. She gathered the clothes and put them in the bin behind the house. "Ain't nuttin like tha' reaaaaaal thang baaaby. Ain't nothing like tha' reaaaaal thang." Harmonious sounds escaping young vocals.

"Whatchu out there sangin' girl?" Memah asked peering from the screen door.

"Nuthin' Mama," was Barbara Jean's ghastly reply. The sense of happiness suddenly begotten.

"Dontchu lie to me chile," Memah said, fiercely making her way down the unstable steps.

Throbbing, but no blood this time. "Yes ma'am," Barbara Jean said weakly as she held her jaw. Memah walked back up the tattered stairs and disappeared into the structure.

"This house bet be clean when we get back," Memah called from inside. Creak. Slam. Silence. Nothingness.

Today was Sunday. Barbara Jean snuck to the edge of the house and peeked around the corner. She watched her mother and her siblings fade down the dirt-paved road. They attended services at the Greater Baptist Church of Monroe. Barbara Jean was always left behind to tend to the chores, Sunday dinner; and daddy.

After they vanished, she continued about washing clothes. Once again, melodic harmony escaping joyous vocals. "Ain't nuthin' like tha' real thang baaaaaaaaby." Shock, fear, panic, terror.

"What'cho mama tell you bout all that sangin' gurl?" Jessie Lee asked. "You know ain't no sangin' 'round hea."

"Yes sir," she said shamefully holding her head down.

"Commere," he summoned.

"Yes sir." No movement.

"You hear me gull? Don't make me take off ma' belt and whip da black offa' you." Anger, power, adrenaline.

"Yes sir." She journeyed towards her father. Fright pierced her sharper than any two-edged sword ever could. Every step felt like quicksand. Head held down, humiliation overshadowing. Pain. Liquid. Unsure of its derivation.

"I said commere. Don't let me tell you again."

"Yes sir." Barbara Jean took the endless journey up the four squeaky stairs; a feeling worse than death.

"Didn't yo' mama tell you ta' wash dem walls in da bafroom?"

"Yes sir." Discomposure overpowered her. No eye contact; except the floor.

"Look at me when I'm talkin' to you," Jessie Lee contended.

"Yes sir." Still, no eye contact. Pain again. Destination unknown. Tears falling like dual tidal waves.

"Dammit, look at me." Jessie Lee grabbed Barbara Jean's face, forcing her to look at him. The thought of looking at him was far worse than the strikes he had just administered to her.

"Whatchu cryin' fo'?" he asked looking straight into her eyes, confirming her terror. He felt dominant and full of control. She could see his eyes turn an evil shade of jet black. It was as if Midnight's son himself had taken over his corpse. His dismal demeanor turned to grimace.

"Please Daddy, no!" Barbara Jean protested. She knew what was to happen next. He forced the top of her head down until she was in proper position. Another sharp pain. No liquid, but the burning in her ear told her the source of her pain.

Her father grabbed both sides of her head and lifted her.

"I'm sorry baby. Daddy sorry. I want you to do that special thang you do for yo' Daddy okay?"

"No Daddy!" Barbara Jean yelped.

Jessie Lee threw her frail body into the wall, her head hitting the sink.

"I wouldn't have ta' do dis' iffen you would jes' do wut I tell you to." Barbara Jean collected enough strength to get up on her knees and take position in front of her father. She unzipped his trousers.

"Thas' right baby. You'z daddy's lil' girl ain'tchu?" Barbara Jean took out her fathers already growing penis and brought her head closer to his crotch.

"I gotta use the bafroom daddy," she pleaded.

"You go to da bafroom when you finish." He pressed her head closer to his penis until the tip was embedded between her lips. Barbara Jean froze. Her father's three-day old sweat overpowered her nostrils. Jessie Lee became angry and thrust his ten-inch organ into her mouth while holding her head in place. Barbara Jean began to choke.

"Dontchu' throw up dis time gotdammit. Dontchu throw up," Jesse Lee demanded. Barbara Jean tried to gasp for air. She could hear her father moaning in such pleasure. Confusion. Pain? Pleasure? Both? His moaning became louder as he tilted his head backwards.

"Yes. Yes. Mmmmmm. Thas' daddy's lil' girl. Yes. Can't nobody make me feel like you can baby girl." Warm liquid invaded her mouth with each continuous moan. His grunts grew louder as if he were a lion about to divulge on its prey.

"Ughhhhhhhrrrrr," escaped him.

Vomit. She rushed to the commode. She missed; liquid rushing out of control.

"Now lookie whatchu done gone and did. Now you gotta clean up dat mess." Jessie Lee retrieved the mop from the kitchen. But she knew her ordeal was far from over.

"Turn ova," he barked. "Take off yo' pannies. I wanna see that pretty lil' pussy of yos'." Barbara Jean didn't move.

"Don't make me do wut I had ta do lass time baby girl. Dontchu' wanna please yo' daddy?"

Jessie Lee put his hands in between her legs and parted them. Barbara Jean was shaking uncontrollably, almost as if she was having a seizure. He touched her warmness through her underwear.

"Yea. Thas' right. You all hot fa' daddy. Thas ma' lil girl." Barbara Jean felt faint as she began to hyperventilate.

"Wus' wrong babygirl?" he asked.

"I can't breath," she panted. Jessie Lee opened the window near the bathtub.

"You be aright. We best hurry up fo' yo' mama 'nem get home. We don't want them knowin' our lil secret do we baby girl?" Silence.

"Do we baby girl?" he raised his voice, holding her face so that her eyes were in contact with his.

"No sir," she said, eyes puffy and red still crying a river.

"Good, now get ova hea ova dis here sink." He bent her over the sink and removed her underwear.

"Gollie, lookie dat sweet lil ass. Yo' mama sho' be jealous if she knew." He propped her chest up over the sink.

"My chest hurt daddy, I can hardly breath."

"Shush up now girl, I'm tryna' concentrate." Sharper pain. He had entered her. Tears; softly, louder. He covered her mouth.

"You shush now. Don't dat feel good? You makin' daddy feel real good now."

She continued crying as the thrusts got harder, deeper and faster. She could vaguely hear her father breathing hard through her own heavy breathing. Her limp body collapsing onto the floor.

"Getcho' ass up. I'm ain't done witchu' yet. Daddy ain't came yet. Getcho' ass back up hea," he yelled. No movement.

"Do you hear me gotdammit? You got ten seconds to getcho' ass up or imma' beat da hell outchu." No movement. He kicked her in the side.

"You makin' daddy really unhappy right now. Get da hell up!" He began to yell hysterically. He kicked her harder and even harder until he realized; fear, panic; she wasn't moving. In fact it didn't look like she was breathing at all.

"Barbara Jean? Barbara Jean? Dontchu' be playin' no games wit me now. You hear me? Ansa me gotdammit!" Nothingness. He picked up her limp body and ran outside to the backyard where the water pump took residence. He doused her with water. No movement.

"Wus wrong Jessie?" he heard Rosie say from the side of the house. Startled, Jessie Lee jumped, dropping Barbara Jean's limp body to the ground.

"She ain't breathin'."

"Whatchu mean she ain't breathin'? Wus wrong wit her?"

"I don't know Rosie, the gurl was out hea' washing clothes and when I looked out hea' ta check on her, she was layin' on da ground."

"Oh Lawd, Jesus, wus wrong with my baby?" Rosie screamed running to her daughter's aid. "What done happened to you? Ansa me girl. Ansa me."

"Imma go get Mr. Reynolds. He know what ta do." Jessie Lee ran past the other children who stood in awe, as he zoomed down the dirt road to Mr. Reynolds' clinic.

"Mista Reynolds, Mista Reynolds," Jessie Lee panted after barging into Dr. Reynolds office. "My baby girl ain't breathin'. She ain't breathin'!"

"Calm down Jessie Lee. What seems to be the problem?" Doctor Reynolds asked.

"My baby girl she ain't breathin'. You gotta come quick. She ain't breathin'. We don't know iffen she dead or alive!"

"Okay. Okay. Jessie Lee. I need you to calm down. Now where is she?"

"Down yonda road at da house," Jessie Lee managed to get out. Dr. Reynolds grabbed his medical bag and he and Jessie Lee drove back to the house.

When they arrived, Jessie Lee jumped out of the car and ran into the backyard where everyone had huddled around Barbara Jean's flaccid body.

"Rosie, Mista Reynolds hea'," Jessie Lee announced.

"Jessie Lee how she get this big ole knot on her head?" Rosie asked. A knot the size of a baseball had appeared on Barbara Jean's forehead.

"I don't know Rosie. Maybe she..she..ummm maybe she uhh.. hit her head on the washin' board."

Dr. Reynolds took out his stethoscope and searched for a heartbeat. "She's still breathing but barely. We need to get her to my office immediately.

"Is she gone be alright?" Rosie asked

"I don't know we have to get her there first. And we need to run some tests on her."

"Whatchu mean run some tests on her?" Jessie Lee asked. Fear reversed. Suspect.

"Well we have to figure out what happened here."

"I done tole you what happened doc. I said she musta fell and hit her head."

"Well we won't know exactly what's wrong until we run those tests Jessie Lee."

Rosie watched in suspicion as Jessie Lee walked back into the house.

††††††

"Mr. and Mrs. Jackson, I've gotten the results back," Dr. Reynolds said a few hours later. Jessie Lee stood up nervously and followed Rosie into Dr. Reynolds' office.

"Is she gone be okay?" Jessie Lee asked.

"In time she will be," he told them; concerned. Suspecting. Jessie Lee let out a sigh of relief and got up to walk out of the office.

"Where you goin'?" Rosie asked him.

"You heard the good docta. She gone be okay."

"She was raped," Dr. Reynolds interrupted. Suspecting.

"Raped?" Rosie asked. Shock, fear, suspecting.

"Whatchu' mean she was raped? How you know she been raped?" Jessie Lee asked. Fearful. Suspect.

"Sit down Mrs. Jackson. Your daughter was raped. The test results show that she suffered severe trauma to her uterus and her pelvis. And it is quite possible she won't be able to bear children."

Rosie began to weep. "Who would do this to my baby?" Nervousness as she already knew and couldn't face; truth.

"She was also beaten real bad. She has two broken ribs, not to mention the large bump on her head," Doctor Reynolds continued. Looking from Rosie to Jessie Lee.

"Since you know err'thang, how she get that?" Jessie Lee asked. Defensive. Suspect.

"She either suffered a hard blow to her head or she suffered a hard fall."

Rosie sat in the chair in front of Dr. Reynolds' desk, looking down at her twiddling thumbs. "Is that all docta?"

"Well, she has a lower lateral cut on the right side of her scull, and a blood clot on her left side. Your daughter was hurt very badly. Do you have any idea who could have done this?" Supsecting.

Rosie didn't speak. She didn't look up. It had gone too far this time.

"I dunno, I mean umm ahh I...I. I don't know doc." Jessie Lee fumbled his words. Suspect.

"Where was she when this happened?" Dr. Reynolds asked them trying another route.

"She was in da back yawd." Jessie Lee answered.

"And where was the rest of the family?" Dr. Reynolds asked trying not to sound accusing.

"I was, um.." Jessie Lee started.

"We was at church," Rosie intercepted. "Thank you docta. Can we take Barbara Jean home now?" Like the other times, there was nothing she could do.

"Unfortunately, Mrs. Jackson, I can't let her go home until I find out if she is pregnant or not. She is in critical condition right now. And if she is pregnant, there's a good chance she won't be able to carry the baby to term." Supsecting.

"Pregnant?" Jessie Lee and Rosie said in unison. Jessie Lee jumped up and began to pace the floor rapidly.

"You are more than welcomed to stay with her. We are going to transfer her to the county hospital up in Baton Rouge." Dr. Reynolds showed great concern and sorrow for Rosie, but his demeanor changed when he looked at Jessie Lee who would not look his way, or Rosie's way for that matter. Suspect.

"How long you thank she gone hafta stay?" Rosie asked.

"A few days if she does well."

Rosie sobbed louder. "Lawd, Lawd, Lawd," was all she said as she rocked back and forth quietly.

"Pregnant?" Jessie Lee repeated, talking to himself as if no one was in the room. Suspect.

"Yes. She was raped severely. Semen was present in her vagina and in her mouth as well as her rectum." Rosie whimpered and quietly walked out of Dr. Reynolds office.

*R*osie was startled by the silhouette approaching the front porch of their old shack. It was Dr. Reynolds. She rocked profusely; for she knew the nature of his visit.

"Jessie Lee. Docta Reynolds hea."

"Good morning Rosie," Dr. Reynolds said peering through the tattered screen door.

"Docta," Rosie acknowledged, nodding her head.

"How you doin' Mista Reynolds?" Jessie Lee asked opening the screen door and inviting the doctor in.

"Well, I wish there was a better reason for my visit Jessie." Dr. Reynolds took off his hat and tilted it towards Rosie before sitting down on the dilapidated sofa opposite her.

Rosie eyed the large envelope that Dr. Reynolds held in his hand. "What's that there you got?" she asked still rocking.

"These are the results of Barbara Jean's pregnancy test."

Rosie's eyes shifted to Jessie Lee. Sweat was pouring from his forehead.

"She pregnant ain't she?" Rosie asked Dr. Reynolds, still studying Jessie Lee.

"Yes Ma'am," he confirmed.

Rosie knew Barbara Jean was pregnant. She had witnessnessed Barbara Jean's change in eating habits and she had missed her period. There were plenty of mornings that Rosie had nursed Barbara Jean as she held the porcelain commode captive.

"Do either of you have any idea who could have done this to Barbara Jean?" Dr. Reynolds asked. One final attempt for the truth to be told. Silence.

A rocking Rosie finally said, "No, I don't reckon we do. Do we Jessie?"

"Naw, I don't reckon we do," Jessie Lee replied holding his head in his hands. "I don't reckon we do."

Chapter 1

I stepped from the shower in the women's locker room of the 24 Hour Fitness on Parker Road. My skin was now wrinkly and a tad bit gray; a sign that I had been in the shower much too long. I hadn't noticed the water's change from the relaxing steamy hot temperature from which it had originated to the lukewarm and undesirable temperature it was now.

I wrapped my purple cotton bath towel around my torso and walked over to the vanity mirror and dropped the towel to the floor. I applied Sesame oil to my skin and began to study my thirty-something shell.

Although I wasn't completely pleased at what I saw in the mirror, I *was* pleased with the progress I had achieved in the effort to reform my body back to its natural state.

As I assessed myself, I tried to figure out at what point in my life I had let myself go. I had always been slim and fit and found myself often times to be the envy of many because I could eat anything I wanted and still look fabulous; even without exercise. It's funny how that works. You go through life thinking that things won't catch up with you and when they do, you're suddenly surprised and by then it's too late.

I chuckled to myself as I thought back to my more *attractive* days. I had entered a short story contest that was posted on Fastweb.com for Playboy Magazine. To this day, I find it hard to believe that I had taken such a bold attitude. I mean, me? Writing an erotic story? No one would have ever expected it; including myself. But I threw caution to the wind and went for it.

The contest called for a fifteen hundred word minimum essay; of course of the erotic genre. I set my pen to paper and was amazed at how my story flowed while I listened to Gerald and Mary J sing *That's The Way I Feel About You*. By the time the CD was over so was my story. First prize was fifteen hundred dollars; need I say more?

Imagine my surprise when three months later the phone rang and one of the editors of Playboy Magazine asked me if I had ever considered posing nude. At first I was offended, until she went on and on about how beautiful I was and how my features were original.

"Not many black women have posed for our magazine. It could be a chance of a lifetime," she said.

"African-American," I corrected her.

"I'm sorry if I offended you," she apologized. But I could sense a little hysteria in her half-assed apology; so much that it even made me laugh. That was her cue that I was okay.

"The bottom line is, no matter what color you are, you're beautiful. And that's what we showcase in our magazine; beautiful women." Had she kept going, my ego would have emerged from my body, hit me on the head and took off down the street

"My mother would kill me if...," I caught what I had said. There I go again trying to please my mother.

"It could prove financially beneficial for you. Six figures may not be a lot to some people but...".

"Six figures?" I asked cutting her off. "Can I get back to you on that?" I was so excited that I nearly forgot the initial reason she had called.

"Take your time. By the way, you are the first prize winner in the contest." She threw that in as though it was merely an after thought.

"Are you serious?" I asked in my best valley girl voice. She gave me the details and told me when I could expect my check. Lord knows I needed that fifteen hundred dollars.

"Give posing some thought," she said before hanging up. I was too through and soaring through the roof. That's why what I did next warranted a beat down.

"Hello?"

"Mama!" I could barely control myself. "I won!"

"Whatchu' talkin' bout?" she asked.

"The writing contest. And they want me to pose for them."

"Who?"

"Playboy!"

"Nekkid?"

"Yes Ma'am. They said they would pay me six figures."

"Have you lost yo gotdamn mind?" She had brought me back to reality. I deserved exactly was I was getting. You would have thought I knew better to even call her and share any kind of joy with her.

"You done already been a damn disgrace to dis' family, and now you wanna go off showin' yo twat to every Tom, Dick and Harry." I sat there and listened to her. As guilt consumed me, I didn't say a word.

"I tell you this. You take off yo' clothes for them white folks and you won't be a part of this family no mo'. You won't hafta *ever* worry bout me talkin' to you no mo'." She hung up.

I sat there for a moment and listened to the buzzing sound coming from the receiver. For the emptiness that I felt at that very moment; even Gerald could not sing it away. I clicked the random button on the CD player. Hmph. Wouldn't you know it; Whitney's "Heart Break Hotel". How fucking convenient. The phone startled me.

"Hello," I answered trying to hide any trace of tears.

"Exactly how much they talkin' bout?" No this bitch did not call me back and ask me that. *Click.*

††††††

I **shook myself** out of my daydream when I heard a couple of women enter the locker room. One was telling the other how she loved her parents who were taking on the responsibility of planning her wedding. Must be nice.

I sat for a moment and listened to their conversation. One told the other that her mother was awesome and she didn't know what she would do with out her. I couldn't comprehend that concept. Tears rolled down my face. For a good relationship with my mother was what I had always longed for.

I put on a long skirt and a halter-top and went to a nearby mirror to douse my tear stained face with cold water. Silence again. The two women were now gone.

"Nasty asses didn't even wash up," I mumbled. I laughed at myself.

I turned to get a side view of myself in the mirror. I admired my dark caramel skin. Although, I wasn't completely where I wanted to be, I was still considered myself sexy. But that wasn't good enough for me. I wanted to be as close to perfect as I could possibly be.

Like they say, we are own worst critic and Mother Time's phlegmatic sense of humor was in no way funny to me. I definitely had plans on showing her up. Her decision to play charades with my body was *effed* up as far as I was concerned. It was on and poppin'. I laughed again. I can't believe I even thought that. I've been hanging around Marlene too much.

Okay, I'm done with my workout today and what I wouldn't give for a bucket of KFC honey BBQ wings right about now. But I won't do that to myself. I was on a mission.

I went downstairs to the cardio room only to find Marlene leaning against a stair master watching the Laker game. Marlene Kelly was my closest friend. Don't ask me why. Most of the time, I felt she was the only one that was benefiting from our relationship.

I guess occasionally when I felt alone she filled some parts of my void. But Marlene was dependent; and I was her enabler. I don't think that Marlene has ever had a real job in her life, yet she lived better than I did.

Marlene was a light skinned sistah that stood five-foot-nine-inches, with a body to die for. She had long pretty hair; the kind that is inevitable when your mother is Hispanic and your father is African-American. If I could think of a song that best described Marlene's abundance in men, I would have to say it was the song by that rapper that sings about having *hoes in different area codes*. His name slips my mind right now.

"Marlene aren't you afraid of catching something from one of these men? Like AIDS; or a *beatdown*?" I had asked her one day during a heated conversation.

"Girl please. If my mama ain't taught me but one thing, she taught me that I'm sittin' on a million dollars." She made a v shape around her pubic area with her hands. I looked at her in confusion. What the hell was that supposed to mean?

I could tell she could sense my incredulousness so she explained. "Girl, you ain't got no kind of street smarts do you? It means that as long as you got pussy, you can get a man to give you anything or *do* anything you want him to do. And my pussy is a pot full of gold."

"That sounds so stupid," I said.

"And that's why you drive what you drive and I drive what I drive. That's why you live where you live and I live where I live. Need I say more?"

She had a point, but the thought was repulsive. "So you think giving yourself to all kinds of men and losing your self respect is worth obtaining material gain?"

"Don't you, of all people, judge me," she snapped.

"I'm not judging you. I just don't see how any self respecting woman could..."

"Don't *even* go there. You *hyyyyyyyypocritical* heffa! You can't even tell your own mother to stay the fuck out of your business. Who the hell are you to question anything I do?" I let it go and never brought it up again.

Marlene was engulfed in the game but I knew that she sensed that I was there even though she didn't make an attempt acknowledge me.

"You're sure not going to lose any weight looking at that television. Who's winning anyway?" I asked.

"Lakers. Up by twelve," she answered not taking her eyes off the television. I wasn't surprised. I had been a loyal Lakers fan since the days of Kareem. In my eyes the Los Angeles Lakers were undefeatable.

"Girl, looking at all that sexy, sweaty flesh running across the screen makes me sweat. I swear I done lost 'bout ten pounds just watchin 'em."

"Sexy? None of those little boys are sexy," I disagreed with her.

"Look at Kobe and Shaq girl. Don't tell me they don't look good.
And then there's that Rick Fox. Hallelujah to me," she said, sounding like
she had just gotten the Holy Ghost.

"Girl please, the only fine man on that screen is playing for the
opposing team."

"Yea and Malone's old ass need to leave Utah and retire before
them white folks hang his ass," she mumbled.

"If he does leave Utah, he'll just go play with the Lakers and make
all those young punks look bad," I joked

"Ain't no way in hell Phil gone let Malone play with the Lakers."
Hands on hips, neck swerving, mouth twisted. Ghetto.

"I really don't care *who* he plays for, just as long as I can continue
to watch him play, with his sexy self," I said to her. She rolled her eyes
at me.

"Anyway. Are you ready to hit the bricks?" I asked. She looked
at me shook her head and laughed.

"What?" I asked. I didn't see what was so funny.

"Nothin'. Let's be out. I can catch the rest of the game at home."

"Ghetto," I mumbled. She shook her head again.

Marlene lit a cigarette once we were in the parking lot. She
always talked about her body being a temple and how she had to take
care of it. Yet she whored around *and* she smoked. I pressed the button
on my key chain to unlock the doors of my Infiniti QX4. Marlene opened
the door.

"It is very apparent that working out causes you to lose *all* sense
of judgment. Because I know you don't think you're about to get your ass
in my car with that cigarette."

"Well lookie, lookie. If it isn't little Miss Christian." She held hand
to her ear as if to make a phone call.

"Yo, yea. What's up Jesus my *faaaaaaaatha*! Yo lissen' here. Yo
girl down here, Ms. High and Mighty, said a curse word and I just thought
you should know. You know, just in case you wanna send some locusts
down here to get her ass."

I looked at her. And wondered how I had associated myself with
someone so ignorant.

"God said ain't no child of His got no business cussin'."

"Saith the morality police," I said rolling my eyes at her.

"Give me a break Renee. You've got your good job. You own
your own place. This fly ride. You got a 401k and stuff. You even got a
good man chasing you, but you ain't tryin' to feel him cause of shit yo
mama planted in you. You look at me like I'm the scum of the earth.
What? I ain't worthy of the same thangs you got?"

"I didn't say all that. You did," was my response. I looked behind me and checked my blind spots making sure it was okay to merge onto I-225. She tried to lighten the mood.

"So what made you want to be a stockbroker anyway? You tryna be like them white folks ain't you?" I shook my head and looked at her. Maybe she didn't know any better.

"Well, after I got my masters," I began to explain to her, "I told myself, I would always be in a position where I would never have to depend on anyone to do anything for me. So the more I thought about it, the more it made sense."

I continued telling her the story of how my former boss, a white man, told me I would be nothing more than a glorified receptionist in his eyes. I can still remember his words when I waltzed into his office one day and asked him for a promotion.

"Walt, I've been here for a while and I'd like to think that I've proven myself. Besides, I am doing the same job that all the new hires are doing. And might I add, you are paying them one hundred twenty thousand dollars a year to start. Yet I'm only making eight dollars an hour."

My confidence wasn't prepared for this short man's response. Walt looked across his large cherry oak desk with his non-charismatic mustache and beady little eyes and said to me, "Renee, all of these women have college degrees."

"I realize that," I interjected. "However, this is a medical slash Internet firm. Most of the new hires hold degrees in something that has nothing to do with their job titles. Now I think fair is fair. I do my job and I do it well; even with my measly associates degree. They come in with fake boobs, short skirts, a degree in home economics or fashion design and you start them at one hundred twenty thousand? That doesn't seem fair to me. Not at all." I could sense his anger and knew he could sense mine. His face turned fire engine red. I could tell he had never had a black person challenge him before.

"Renee, let me say this to you in the best way I know how." He put his hands together, placed his elbows on his desk and leaned forward. "*Without* your bachelors, your masters or your doctorate, all you will *ever* be at this company is a glorified receptionist."

I looked at him and a part of me wanted to reach across his desk and slap that stupid smirk off his unsightly face. I even envisioned pulling out an oozie and shooting him right in the middle of his forehead. Racist asshole. No, I'll pass. This man just told me in so many words that I would not be anything without that piece of paper or as long as I was black. Part of me felt that he was right. I was a black woman in Colorado; in Corporate America. No, I'd do him one better.

I stood up and put a fake smile on my face. "Thank you Walt. That was the nicest thing any racist has ever said to me. I thank you for your honesty."

He looked at me perplexed. I thanked him for his words of wisdom, shook his hand, turned and walked out of his office. I held my fabricated smile as I claimed the few personal possessions I owned from my desk on my way out the door. I didn't even turn around to see his expression. Bastard.

After I left, I drove my Hyundai Sonata straight to the University of Phoenix and enrolled in their Bachelor's of Information Technology Sciences program. I already had my Associates degree in Computer Science, so obtaining my bachelor's would be a breeze.

In a crucial attempt to improve myself, I left the university and headed straight to 24 Hour Fitness to sign up. I hired a trainer and was put on an individualized diet plan. I promised myself I would loose the extra weight that had claimed the real me. So now I am in the gym nearly six days a week. I'm glad I did it. Although I was currently a whopping one hundred fifty-five pounds, it was far better than the two hundred fifty pounds I was some short months before.

"That's why you ain't got on man." Marlene interrupted me.

"Right. Like that fine upstanding man you've been taking care of."

"At least I got one," she retorted. "You want too much and everything has to be so perfect. You ain't even perfect yo'self."

"Whateva trick." I dropped her off at her apartment in Montebello and stopped by King Soopers to get a few groceries. It was a nice sunny evening and the weather was just right. It was kind of unusual for Colorado weather. Here, it was either too cold or too hot.

I picked up some Summer's Eve, cocoa butter, some fresh fruit, some chicken breasts, lettuce, safflower oil and some baking soda and headed back to my condo.

I was somewhat bothered by what Marlene had said earlier. She wasn't too far off. The likelihood of me having a successful relationship was not in the cards. In the last two years, I had been in so many relationships I had lost count. My quest for Mr. Right always turned up Mr. Everything Is Wrong.

My relationships usually had a short livelihood ending in record time than the previous. I know it sounds bad but it doesn't take me long to realize whether or not I want to put up with a man. When that first red flag goes up, no matter how minor, I'm ghost or he's got to go.

After Randy, I vowed that I would never date men my age ever again. Randy, although five years my senior, was immature, irresponsible and just a plain old pain in my ass. After him I raised my age requirement to forty.

"Girl, you crazy," Marlene teased. "So how old is too old for you?" she asked.

"Just as long as they are between the ages of forty and fifty-five, that's okay with me."

"Girl you like them with one foot in the grave don't you?" she teased. "I guess those social security benefits will come in handy." She looked at me shaking her head, "I don't like nothin' old but money."

My mother was constantly nagging me about giving her grandchildren. For the life of me I don't know why. She should have been happy with the abuse she bestowed upon me. Besides, she didn't even like children.

"You ain't gettin' no younger," she had told me. "If you don't find you a man soon, you might as well forget it. You need ta stop being so picky. You ain't no prize yo'self."

She made a habit of putting me down in an attempt to destroy my self-esteem and I must admit, at times, she succeeded. She was the reason I had gained so much weight. She was always telling me that I was too skinny and ugly, and that I would end up having baby after baby, supporting them on welfare. What a thing to tell your daughter.

I wasn't ready to have children yet. To tell you the truth, I don't think I even want any. The way I see it, they just may turn out to be as screwed up as I was. And I certainly was not going to have a child and then turn around and raise it alone because the some sorry ass black man decided it wasn't time to grow up *and* left me to take care of little Johnny on my own.

Yes indeedy, I had lost sight of the fairy tale of Mr. Right coming to my aid and falling in love, sweeping me off my feet and living happily ever after. Wait. Which comes first the sweeping off the feet and then falling in love or the other way around? Oh well. It doesn't matter anyway. I was convinced things like that only happened in the movies.

Actually, in complete contradiction, my knight in shining armor *had* come into my life. He had come in the form of Charlie Thatcher. Charlie was a forty-seven year old white male, who happened to be president of options trading at Charles Schwab; the firm where we both worked. I know, it's confusing right?

Well, as much as I tried to deny it, I truly loved Charlie but the biggest issue that I had with him was his race. The fact that he was white really complicated things for me. Being the stubborn soul that I was, I refused to deal with the racial drama that I had witnessed with other interracial couples. My mother had taught me that black folks don't "sleep with the enemy". I guess someone failed to tell the 'black man'.

When I was young, my mother had done a half assed job of conditioning me to hate white people and categorize them as being devils. I often asked her if that was the case, why was it okay for black men to engage in intimacy with white women. Her response was "Niggas choose to be wit' white trash 'cause they thank us black women folk ain't worth shit. And if our own men don't thank we is shit why in da hell you thank a white man would wanna be with one a us?" She would say that if a white man acted interested in a black woman, it would only be because he wanted a piece of ass; and only in private.

"Den one day if you piss him off, he gone slip up and call you a nigga'. And his family ain't gone neva accept you. You thank he gone give up his family for a nigga? Hmph. I don't think so."

It took me a while to understand that my mother was angry and bitter. She told me that my father had left her for a white woman and gave that woman everything that my mother only dreamed of. She never had a good thing to say about a black man. And I can't say that I blamed her then too much. The examples that I was exposed to gave me more than enough proof to validate her statement.

Even in this day and age, things that she had taught me about black men were still evident. If the high percentage of black men in the judicial system wasn't depressing enough, the jobless rate and single mother numbers added icing to the cake. And then comes the story of the down low brother. Damn shame. Because of this I was harder on men; black men, than I should have been. I had a certain criteria for men I would associate with. He had to be educated, mature, handsome, financially stable, own his own car, own his own home, dabble in the stock market, be extremely intelligent, packing at least nine inches, know how to use that nine inches, know what foreplay was, possess common sense and be willing to treat me like a queen. Whew, that was a mouthful. Sue me.

When I was out and about, I studied and watched interracial couples. I observed the looks they received when in public. I heard the way people talked behind their backs. I saw how their mixed-race children were mistreated. I knew how families would disown them for not sticking with their own. I wasn't so naïve to believe that racism was a thing of the past. All of it depressed me and discouraged me. And if that didn't put a damper on things, my place in society did.

††††††

When I got to my front door I could hear my answering machine beeping. Once inside, I place the grocery bags on the counter and pressed the message retrieval button.

You have three new messages in your mailbox. Message one, left today at 9:54 a.m. "Renee, this is your mother. Call me when you get in. I need to go to the store." She must have had company because she was trying her best to be sidditified.

Message two left today at 1:57p.m. "Renee where you? I been waitin' on yo' ass all day." Company must be gone. *Message three left today at 2:05 p.m.* Click. I knew that one was my mother; again. I swear she is driving me crazy.

My mother knew how to get under my skin. She acted as if I sat home all day waiting to jump at her every beck and call. Just as I was getting ready to call her, the phone rang.

"Hello Mama," I said, knowing that it was her on the other end..

"Renee, where the hell you been?"

"I just .."

"You don't think about no damn body but yo'self," she blurted before I could get a word in edgewise.

"Mama do you still need to go to the store?" I asked, trying to hurry the conversation along.

"I needed to go to the damn store a long time ago."

"Look Mama, I'm tired, and I don't feel like arguing with you tonight. Do you need to go to the store or not?"

"You act like you...," was all I let her get out.

"Mama, do me a favor and call me when you want to go to the store. Or call Eddie. I really don't feel like hearing it tonight." I didn't give her a chance to say anything else. I just hung up the phone.

Everyone had that great, big, sharp, excruciating, painful thorn in their ass. You know, that thorn that kept them down, that thorn that pricked and pricked, putting them into a deep depression and made you either contemplate suicide; or murder. My thorn was my mother; Barbara Jean Jackson.

Even at four-foot-eleven, she always had a way of making me feel smaller; like I was nothing. She constantly reminded my brother Eddie and I how we ruined her life. She told us that she could have been something back in the day if she hadn't made the mistake of getting pregnant. She said back then, they didn't believe in abortions.

"'Cause if they did, yall sorry asses wouldn't be here," she told us several times. She said she was ignorant when she got pregnant with me and stupid when she got pregnant with Eddie.

I retorted telling her, "No, Mama, we would be here had you kept your legs closed and you hadn't given it up to every soldier up in that Army base." Each time I said it, she would slap me. I didn't care. I wanted her to see how much it hurt when she said shit like that. I've never seen a mother hate her children the way my mother did. Albeit her despise for her children had a different effect on Eddie than it did I. While I was starving for my mother's love and attention and tried everything I could think of pleasing her, Eddie's approach was much different.

At the age of fourteen, Eddie got involved in gangs and drugs and dropped out of school. I didn't know what a Crip was until Eddie ended up in the hospital one day after being beat so badly; the first part of his initiation. What baffled me the most was even though Eddie was on path to destruction, my mother had no problem showing him love. When he needed her, she was there. I could never count on the same. And even though she would refer to both of us in a negative light when we were together, I had secretly observed that Eddie was her favorite and she would literally kill anyone that hurt him. I guess this added to my list of excuses to why I never finished anything I started.

I started college, straight out of high school and *just* completed my masters two years ago. Here we are several years later and I am just now finishing up my doctorate.

I remember the year after I had graduated high school; I had started working on my degree in Computer Science. Along with going to school, I held down a full time job. Living with my mother, I had to pay half the rent, half the utilities, *my* phone bill, *her* phone bill *and* give her a little spending cash.

One day, the first installment of the student grant that I had applied for came through. It happened to be on the same day that I got my paycheck. Trying to please my mother, I decided that I would give her my entire paycheck and keep the money from the student grant.

"Mama after work today, can I go over to Gary's house?" I had asked her.

"Don't you get paid today?" she asked me.

"Yes ma'am. I will go cash my check after work then bring you the money."

"Okay, then I guess you can go." She didn't know at the time that I had the grant money in tow.

When I got off work that day, I went to the bank, cashed my check and took the money to my mother. She was so happy to get the money that she completely forgot that I was standing there as she walked away counting the money.

Gary was secretly my boyfriend. We had been secretly dating since grade school. I would have never told my mother because if she knew, she would make sure that I never saw him again. So to her, he was just a classmate.

Gary lived with his parents and a slew of brothers and sisters. On this particular day, we decided that we didn't want to be watched every minute that we were together. Ten brothers and sisters, tons of nieces and nephews, and his mother and father occupied the four bedroom ranch style home; not my idea of a romantic date. We decided to head out for a night on the town.

After driving for a while, we settled on a mall up North. Northglenn Mall I believe. We were at the mall all but forty-five minutes into our browsing, when I was paged over the loudspeaker.

"Renee Matthews, please come to the information booth located in the center of the mall. You have an emergency phone call." I was puzzled because we didn't tell anyone where we were going, and even if we had slipped and said we were going to the mall, there were at least five we could have chosen from.

"I wonder who that is," I told Gary, completely baffled. When I got the information desk, I told the clerk who I was, and she handed me the phone.

"Hello?"

"Get your black ass home right now! I'm going to beat the shit out of you!" It was my mother. I didn't dare disrespect her and ask her why.

Gary took me home as we rode in silence. I was embarrassed, scared and not to mention had this nervousness in the pit of my stomach that brought on a serious case of nausea.

Forty minutes later we sat silently in the car in front of my mother's townhouse. Gary stared at me helplessly and rubbed my shoulder. He sensed my trepidation and offered to walk me inside. I should have known better thinking that letting Gary come inside my mother's home would soften my blow. It only angered my mother more.

When I got inside the door, I didn't even have a chance to close it before she came at me with the extension cord. She hit me wherever the cord would land.

"Yo' ass thought you was slick," she said in between swings. "Where's that damn money you got from yo' school today? I want *all* of it." I looked mystified, wondering how in the world she found out that I had gotten the money. Then it occurred to me that my aunt, who also attended the same college as I, must have gotten her grant money and had called my mother to find out if I had gotten mine.

After my mother beat me, and she was satisfied with the amount of blood oozing from my battered body, I handed her what I had left of the money. I had bought a dress and a keyboard; both costing sixty dollars all together. I handed her the nine hundred fifty dollars that I had left.

"You can leave now. You don't change a damn thang round here buddy," my mother told Gary. Gary looked at me with a tear in his eye as open welts on my skin drizzled blood. He wiped blood from one on my face that clotted as soon as it discharged. His eyes said he was sorry and goodnight. I knew if he could or even if he knew how, Gary would rescue me from this iniquity.

After Gary had departed, my mother started in on me again; hitting me with the extension cord. I dare not move. The pain was excruciating, but not as painful as the hurt I felt in my heart. My own mother treated me as if I was some trash from the street and she had embarrassed me; in front of my boyfriend.

"You thank you slick. Don't you *ever* try to keep nothin' from me. I'll kill yo' black ass just as sho as you standin' there!"

"Yes ma'am," I said, holding my head low. Once she excused me, I went to my room and put my head under my pillow so she wouldn't hear me crying. Had she heard me, she would have come back for more.

I began to pray but was interrupted by my concern as to why God had left me to fend on my own. Why hadn't He intervened? I knew God existed. He had to. That's what we learn in church; that God is ever present and that He can make a way out of no way. He's our rock, our salvation. Right?

Well, where was God when my Paw Paw was murdered? Where was God when my Uncle raped me? Where was God, when my mother mistreated me every chance she got? Then I started to wonder why He didn't just let her kill me and get it over with.

At that very moment, death was an option for me; so much that on that very night I contemplated suicide. My psyche scanned every part of our house. Where could I get some pills to overdose on? My mother had plenty of pills, but they were in her room. That zone was forbidden to me. I could slice my writs, but I would be too chicken to sit there and actually cut my own wrist and watch the blood flow from my body.

I went into the bathroom, shutting the door behind me. I looked in the cabinet under the sink. Damn; only ammonia and Pine Sol. I read the labels of both. *Harmful if swallowed.* I took a guzzle of both and went back into my room and shut the door.

I lay in my bed waiting for the unthinkable to happen. Soon I would have to endure pain no more. I would be gone from this place and drift to a place of serenity. I had heard songs and read books about the streets of Heaven being paved with gold and overflowing with milk and honey. And at this very moment that is exactly where I wanted to be.

A few minutes later, I sprinted to the bathroom; vomit barely making the toilet. I wasn't finding God's sense of humor the least bit amusing. My mother didn't even bother to ask if I was okay. All she said was, "You bet not be pregnant."

God had forsaken me yet again, and I would have to live to suffer

the torture of another day. That night, I cried myself to sleep.

Chapter 2

I **examined my** apartment. I think I'll stay in tonight, turn on some Angelo and Veronica and just sit here on the floor in the dark. The red light was flashing on the phone. I had two more messages. How I missed them, I don't know.

Message one, left today at 6:55 p.m. "Aye boo, iss' me, I thought maybe you'd wanna come by and watch the game wit' me. Cawl me when you get home. Love you."

That was Kevin's country ass. He was starting to irk the hell out of me.   I met Kevin through Marlene. I think that's pretty much self-explanatory. I did it as a favor for her and her boyfriend.

"Just go out with him and see what happens," Marlene pleaded.

"Kevin is one of the few good guys left," her boyfriend chimed in. "He needs a good woman that's about somethin' and goin' somewhere." You've got to be friggin' kidding. *Aaaand* I was the first the first person they thought of?

On our first date, he was an hour late and then his black ass pretended like he left his wallet at home when we got ready to leave the restaurant. I did him one up. I took a credit card from my wallet and told Kevin to pay for dinner as I excused myself to the ladies room.

"Order dessert too," I told him and kissed him on the cheek. "I just *looove* strawberry cheesecake," I seductively whispered in his ear. I left his dumb ass sitting there and walked right out of the restaurant. When I got home, I called the credit card company and reported my credit card stolen.

I knew right away that longevity would not be on our side. All he ever talked about was how he was going to get married and have a house full of kids while he supported them on two jobs as a janitor. *Not with me he wasn't.* I told him on several occasions not to ever call me, but he insisted that I was playing hard to get.

"Renee, just give him a chance. You know it takes a good woman to bring out the good in a man." I was starting to think I was as desperate as Marlene was.   It amazed me what she would do for a piece of warm dick. Her boyfriend was cheating on her in every sense of the word and used her every chance he got. She used that old 'stand by your man' viewpoint.   Well my viewpoint is more like kick his broke, good for nothing, dumb ass to the curb and get a friggen' clue.

Message two, left today at 7:15 p.m. "Aye boo, is' me again. When you come by, can you brang a twelve-pack wit'chu? Love you." Bastard.

Damn. My phone rang again. I have to get my number changed. This is ridiculous.

"Hello?" I answered. Don't ask me why I answered it.

"Renee?" The female voice was one that I had never heard before.

"Yes?"

"How are you?"

"Fine. Who is this?" I asked.

"This is Linda, Kevin's mama." She acted as if I was supposed to know who she was.

"Oh hello Mrs. Taylor. How are you today?" Phony as hell.

"Oh girl, I'm blessed. Lookie here, I was preparin' the menu for Thanksgivin' and wanted to know if there was anythang you wanted specially prepared?"

"Huh?" I asked taken off guard.

"For Thanksgivin' dinner. I'm making the menu out now as we speak," she said.

"I'm sorry Mrs. Taylor, I had no idea you were inviting me to dinner. I had planned on spending Thanksgiving with my mother," I lied.

"Oh?" she said puzzled. "Well I spoke ta Kevin earlier and he said yall was spendin' Thanksgivin' wit us." That fucker. It's time to make sure he gets the message that I don't want much of anything to do with his sorry ass.

"I'm sorry, maybe Kevin was confused, but I will spending Thanksgiving at my mother's this year," I repeated. "But I do appreciate you inviting me."

"Well, uh, okay," she said sounding just as confused as I did. "If you change yo' mind, you more than welcomed. There's gone be more than enough food. Besides the whole family would love to spend more time gettin' to know our future in-law." See, hell no. Kevin thought he was slick, but I was about to show him that I was the wrong one to be fucking with.

"Thank you Mrs. Taylor," I said in a fake tone. "If I don't see you then, Happy Thanksgiving."

"You too baby," she said, with uncertainty in her voice.

I hung up the phone. Everything down to the fact that his name was Kevin just irked my very being. I was one of those women who had always downed other women for taking stupid shit from men and letting them get away with it. Right now I was no different. And from the outside I was looking really pathetic.

I was sick of the phone ringing, so I decided to turn the ringer off. If my mother wanted to go to the store, she'd have to wait until tomorrow.

When I reached for the phone, it rang.   Shit.   For some stupid reason, I answered it anyway; again; my nosey ass.

"Hello?" I said blandly.

"Girl, you goin' out tonight?" It was Marlene.

"No, I think I'm going to spend some quiet time in tonight."

"You sure? I went to this club called Bernard's last weekend girl.   It's over there off 37th and Peoria and *girllll* there were some fine niggas up in there!"

"Niggas?" I asked.   "You know I don't do niggas."

"You know what I mean heffa.   Brothas."

"Then call them brothas and stop calling them niggas.   You'd be mad as hell if a white person called you a nigga."

"You damn right.   They better not ever call me that to my face."

"Ignorant," I mumbled.

She was silent for a moment before she said, "What's wrong with you Renee?"

"Nothing Marlene, I just want to be alone right now is all.   You go ahead to the club and have fun okay?"

"Well, okay.   I'll talk to you tomorrow."

"Marlene?"

"Yea?"

"Be careful," I said apprehensively.   Marlene was an accident waiting to happen.   She had come up pregnant before by someone she had a one-night stand with and had nerve to ask me for the money for an abortion.   She wasn't committing murder with my hard earned money.   She eventually got the money from her parents.   If her boyfriend found out he would surely kick her ass; again.

"Girl I'm always safe.   Got four friends named Trojan Extra Rippled to protect me," she giggled.

"Bye hoe," I said and hung up.   I turned off the ringer before anyone else could call.   I made sure the doors were locked and the shades were drawn.

After grabbing a bottle of Moscato, I turned off the lights, flipped the play button on the CD player and sat on the floor in front of it.   Tonight, I wanted to be in my own little world.   I decided against Angelo and Veronica and went for some Gerald Levert.   No one can place you into another world like Gerald.

I drank a couple of glasses of Moscato, but all it did was give me a light buzz.   I remembered that Marlene had left a bottle of Christian Brothers the last time she was by.   That stuff is so strong, and she drank it like water.   Although I hadn't looked, I was sure Marlene had a few hairs on her chest.

I retrieved the half empty bottle from the cabinet and a Coke from the fridge and returned to my place in front of the stereo. I lit a lilac candle and as I drank the brandy, glared into the candle's flames as Gerald sang *Love and Consequences* to me.

The room started spinning, and soon I was in a world that brought back every pain that I had ever encountered. I cried. I drank. I cried harder. I drank more. Slowly. Painfully. Creeping. Backwards. Memory lane. Distant past. I drifted.

"*Jesus is on the main line. Tell him what you want. Ohhh. Jesus is on, the main line. Tell him what you want. Jesus is on, the main line. Tell him what you want. You just call him up and tell him, what you want.*" I was off key. I didn't care. I didn't want to come to choir rehearsal anyway. I didn't like singing, but Mama made me come anyway.

"You keep trying to sing soprano, but you're an alto," Sister Alice had told me. It made no difference to me one way or the other. I would have rather been on the phone yapping with Gary. My mother only came so she could have ample time to flirt with all the men in the church at closer range. She once told the first lady that she was just waiting for her to slip, because when she did, she was going to take her man. My mother exuded the confidence that she had pilfered from me.

I surveyed the church, searching for my mother and her *next* victim. When I spotted her, she was at the back of the church with Mother Alexander.

Mother Alexander was hugging my mother as my mother buried her face in her hands. Something wasn't right. Mother Alexander's gaze caught mine, and she motioned with her hand for Eddie and I to come to the back of the church. I complied. I took Eddie by the hand as we made our way in their direction; my balance somewhat wobbly.

"What's wrong?" I asked. My mother was snotting up a storm and if I didn't know any better she was going for an academy award for best nervous breakdown. Eddie stood and watched silently. He rarely showed emotion, but supported my mother by shifting her face from Mother Alexander's mucus stained shoulder to his.

"Your grandfather has been killed," Mother Alexander told us. My heart skipped a few beats. I felt as if my chest had caved in. Surely I had heard her wrong.

"Ma'am?" I asked for clarification. Eddie looked at me as if to say 'not you too'. I rolled my **eyes at** him.

Mother Alexander looked at me, for she knew I was about to go into shock. She didn't repeat what she had just told me. She didn't need to.

The sadness and regret in her eyes confirmed that what I had heard her say was indeed correct.

I screamed; nothing came out. *I* could hear it, but no one else did. My mother sobbed louder. By now we had the attention of the entire church. Sister Alice tried to divert their attention.

"Okay let's take it from the top," she told the choir. Her attempts were all but successful.

Between the waterworks that came from the three of us, Moses could have certainly led an army across the river they created.

Later that night, we would leave Denver by car, headed for Baton Rouge where my grandfather had resided. We would be riding with my great uncle Melvin and the drive take about fifteen hours. Fifteen hours with my mother, my brother, my great uncle Melvin, my mother's oxygen tank and uncle Lenny; the man with the wandering hands. All in a Cadillac Coupe De Ville. It was going to be a long drive.

My uncle Lenny hardly ever said much, I later found out he spoke more with his actions than any words he could ever speak. His need to touch things that had no business touching made me his next prey. On occasion his hands wandered and found asylum on my thigh. After shooing him away a few times and him not getting the picture, I tapped my mother on the shoulder.

"Mama," I whispered, "Uncle Lenny keeps..."

"I can't believe you," she scolded me. "My Daddy just died and all you can do is thank about yo'self." You've got to be kidding. Truth be told, Paw Paw and I were closer than he and my mother *ever* were. And although it baffled me, I could never make the connection as to why. Hell, I was closer to my Paw Paw than *any* of his children. Paw Paw protected me from a many a whippings, those that I did and did not deserve.

I leaned back in my seat and tried to scoot as far away from Uncle Lenny as possible; not that it helped much. Situation had it that I had to sit between he and Eddie.

††††††

We **turned into** the parking lot of my Paw Paw's apartment complex a record twelve hours later. There were lots of people standing around; people that I didn't know. Who were these people? Either they were bystanders, or Paw Paw had *lots* of friends. Much to my surprise everyone knew who my mother and I were. No one seemed to remember Eddie.

"Barbara Jean, I'm so sorry baby. Jessie Lee was a good man," one would say.

"There's his little girl, Renee. Girl all your grandaddy ever did was talk aboutchu'," another said. I looked from Eddie to my mother. I did not remember any of these faces.

I noticed a group of spectators standing a few feet away from us looking down at a patch of dark grass in front of them that looked like oil from where I was standing.

"Here go his blood. He got smoked right here," one of them said. I looked horrified. How could they?

"That's where it happened," one woman told me, pointing in the direction of the spectators. Later I found out her name was Mary Lou. "He shot him right there. Nonsense. For a bottle of likka."

I walked over to the blood stained grass that became evident the closer I got.

"Get away from here!" I screamed. "Respect my Paw Paw!" I shooed everyone away from the spot, and wondered why the police hadn't cleaned up the blood. It was as if they had left there on purpose; a tribute to my grandfather.

"Baby you need to go up and lay down. You don't need to be upset right now." That was Mary Lou. I looked up at the window that was the living room to my grandfather's apartment. There was no way that I was going up there. I couldn't. My attention reverted from the window to a conversation I heard a few feet behind me.

"What happened to my daddy?" I heard my mother ask an unknown woman, whom I later found out was my grandfather's mistress, Lula Mae. Did everyone's name here end with Mae?

"Yo' daddy and Chuck was playin' dominos and we don't kno' who was winnin' fo' real, but I thank yo' daddy was. Chuck said Jessie Lee was cheatin' and when he won the game, Jessie Lee told Chuck to pass 'em the bottla' shank that he had won." I later found out shank was a bottle of expensive whiskey.

"When Chuck passed it to Jessie Lee, he dropped it," she continued. "Chuck got mad and started yellin' at Jessie Lee 'bout all tha thangs he had to do ta get that bottla likka."

I looked Lula in her age decrepit face and wondered what my Paw Paw saw in her. She was a lot taller than my Memah, but she wasn't as attractive. She was black as night and I could count the teeth in her mouth on one hand, and even those were a dark shade of yellow. She had pretty hair, but that was the only attractive feature I could find on her; that and the fact that she seemed to be real nice. I had never forgiven Memah for causing my Paw Paw to leave and move back to Longview. I felt had my grandfather not left, my life would have been much different and my Paw Paw would still be alive. I tuned back into what Lulu was saying.

"Chuck tole Jessie Lee to hold on, said he had somethin' for his ass and he rolled out the apartment."

I was puzzled. "Rolled?" I asked.

"Yes chile. Chuck is a paraple...a paraplee..."

"Paraplegic," I helped her.

"Yea, and he got around in a wheel chair." None of this made sense to me. Paw Paw lived on the second floor and Chuck lived downstairs on the ground floor.

"When Chuck came back, he shot yo' daddy with his sawed off shot gun."

At this point, I was even more confused than I was before. I tried to put the pieces together. I could understand the fact that Chuck was mad that he lost to my Paw Paw in dominos, and that Paw Paw broke his bottle of liquor. What I was having the hard time with was how Chuck got back and forth from the bottom and top floors if he was in a wheelchair and Lulu's story about Chuck coming back into the apartment and shooting my Paw Paw. If that was the case, where did this big blotch of blood that I was standing in front of come from? I looked at Lulu in suspicion.

"Renee, get your fass tail up in here and set up my oxygen tank!" my mother yelled from the window. I hadn't seen her go up the stairs. I looked around and didn't see Eddie either. Why didn't she call him? I briefly diverted my attention to the mini-van that entered the driveway and parked in the parking lot. It didn't look familiar; not until I saw Memah get out. I held my head and rolled my eyes. Oh Lord, let the drama begin. I looked back up at the window that my mother had just yelled to me from and saw Eddie's silhouette in the window.

Please Lord don't make me go up there. I couldn't disobey my mother, I'd surely get a whipping then. I debated on whether that was a whipping that I would gladly take. I thought against it. I went upstairs and scanned the entrance to the apartment. *How the hell did Chuck get up these two flights of stair?* still rang in my mind. I looked around my grandfather's apartment once I finally choked up enough nerve to go inside.

The apartment was small. Paw Paw had an old gold couch, a brown reclining chair and a dark wooden coffee table. In the makeshift dining area he had a card table and three chairs. The kitchen area was almost non-existent. It consisted of a small sink, stove, and fridge that came to my chest. I went into the bedroom and sat on his bed. I wanted to feel his presence. I was unsuccessful.

"What's takin' you so long? Don't have me beat yo' ass the first night we here," my mother said from the other room. I gathered her cord and took it to her. I watched her continue her quest for best actress in a leading role as she pretended like she was having a hard time breathing. I must admit, she was *good*.

Lights. Action. Camera! Memah walked in the apartment with my aunt Lena. I looked at Eddie and without words we were both in agreement as to how this scene would play out.

"I can't believe that ugly ho had the nerve to brang her ugly ass around hea'. Jessie Lee still my husband. She ain't got no right to be here."

"You know Rosie, I ain't gone fight with you right now. My beloved Jessie Lee 'bout to be sent home six feet unda and I ain't gone let you get my pressure up." Memah hadn't seen Lula Mae walk up behind her and the look on Memah's face was priceless when she realized that Lula Mae had heard what she had said. I looked over at Eddie again and raise an eyebrow. He tilted his head. Once more without words Eddie told me *you know black folks can't have no funeral without no fighting*. I smiled. He smiled back.

"I knew Jessie Lee was gone die behind some triflin' woman." Memah shot at Lula Mae.

"That ain't true Rosie 'cause he left you. You memba? Thas why he leff you. Dontchu be angry wit me 'cause I ain't break up yo marriage. *You* broke up yo marriage not me. You ain't know how to treat yo' man. I may not be the prettiest thang but betchu dis much, Jessie Lee loved him some Lula Mae. That's one thang I know fa sho'." I knew it was about to get ugly.

Memah dropped her purse on the floor and lunged at Lula Mae. Eddie jumped up and made himself a partition between the two women.

"Both yall need to chill the fuck out," he said. Oh Lord, what did he do that for, because my Academy Award winning mother started the waterworks again.

"Why yall disrespectin' my daddy like this fo'?"

"Barbara Jean, shut the hell up," Memah told her.

"You need to watch how you speak to my mama," Eddie told her. Umph, Umph, Umph. My Paw Paw isn't even here and he done started World War III up in here.

Another one of my mother's sisters ran into the apartment with a broom and aimed for straight for Eddie. It caught him on the side of his face. Eddie grabbed her by her neck and slapped her.

"What the fuck is yo' problem?" he asked her.

"Let her go Eddie," my mother told him. But I knew it was going to take more than her telling him once to let my aunt go. I could see the rage in his eyes. The killer in him had re-emerged.

"Bitch, if you ever put your hands on me, my mama or my sister again, I will kill your ass."

"Eddie!" my mother yelled louder. I stood in the farthest corner of the living room and watched in amazement. These fools are acting crazy and this wasn't even about them. I made my way around all of them; around all of the yelling and cursing; around all of the crying and around all of the physical displays of dislike and hatred and went back into my grandfather's room and sat on his bed.

No one including myself saw Uncle Lenny slither in. He too made his way around the Hollywood production and glided into my Paw Paw's room. I panicked. I didn't know what to do. He sat on the bed next to me and put his arm around my shoulders.

"How you holdin' up babygirl?" he asked me. I didn't say anything. I tried scooting further away from him but he followed me.

"I ain't gone bite you," he said; his hand moving further down my back. His fingers snapping the top of my underwear caused me to jump straight up.

"Leave me alone or I'm going to tell!"

"Sit down girl," the evil stench of his grin still on his face. "This will be our lil' secret. Ain't nobody gotta know. You do me a favor and I do you a favor. You know, kinda like friends do."

This disgusting replica of a man must think that I am really stupid. He was smooth and it was clear that he had done this before. Incest ran in our family, and much to my surprise, everyone was okay with it. I had aunts and cousins who were also brother and sister. Yes my genealogy held many dark secrets and many dark tales.

"I'm going to tell my mama on you," I told him.

He chuckled, "You know she ain't gone believe you." I went into the living room.

"Mama!" No response. "Mama!" I attempted again.

"Get the hell of my face!" she finally said. I looked back at Uncle Lenny who stood in the doorway of my grandfather's bedroom with a heckling grin on his face. Tears began falling from my eyes. I didn't know what to do, but I knew I couldn't stay in here. I hid in the rental van that Memah and my aunts had traveled in. I stayed there for hours and eventually drifted off to sleep.

I was awakened by Eddie who slide the side door open and said, "Mama want you."

The day of the funeral was the hardest for me. When they lowered my Paw Paw into the ground, my aunts had to hold me back from jumping in with him. I wanted to see him one last time. It was a closed casket service. The blow to his chest from the sawed off shotgun, tore my grandfather up so that it nearly severed his body in half. The local newspaper a few days earlier read: *Longview man murdered by a disabled man over a bottle of alcohol.* That day was the end of the rest of my life.

We returned to Denver two days after my grandfather's funeral. After fifteen hours of roving hands, the inevitable happened. I still remember that God awful night just like it was yesterday.

My mother wasn't too happy that I didn't play supporting actress in her role. That day Eddie and I had argued about how stupid everyone acted at the funeral. My mother became enraged, reminded of how much of a disappointment I was to her and put me out. She knew I had nowhere to go except to Memah's house. And she knew that without finance, I wouldn't be able to *stay* at Memah's house. Even knowing this, I headed to her house anyway.

"What Barbara Jean done did now," my grandmother said when she opened her front door after I knocked on it.

"She put me out."

"Fo' what dis time?"

"Arguing with Eddie about the funeral," I said walking into her kitchen to see if she had cooked.

"It's some greens, cornbread and some pig feet in dere," she said already knowing what I was in search for.

"I was telling Eddie that it didn't make any sense that we shamed Paw Paw the way we did. And mama got mad and put me out."

"I don't know wus wrong wit dat chile."

I nodded my head and agreed with everything regardless of what she said. I was hungry and those greens were awesome. She can keep the pig feet. A few minutes later we were both interrupted by a knock at the door.

"Yes Suh?" My grandmother asked the officer when she opened the door.

"Ma'am, my name is Officer Malloy. Do you know a Renee Matthews?" he asked her. My half-pint grandmother put her hand on her hip and tilted her head.

"Yes suh. She my granddaughter. Is there a problem officer?" Sassiness written all over her demeanor.

"Yes. She was reported as a runaway by her mother."

"She ain't run away. Her mama put her out like she always do when she get mad."

My grandmother invited the police officer in and told him to take a seat.

"Have something to drink?" she offered.

"No thank you," he declined.

My grandmother explained to the officer my mother's constant abuse and told her how she resorted to putting me out when she was tired of me.

"Well ma'am, I admire your concern for your granddaughter, but her mother *has* reported her as a runaway." He shifted onto his right knee. "Technically, if we knew where she was, we would have to take her back home. On the other hand," he said in a reassuring tone, "if we don't know where she is, then we can't take her back." He paused for a moment, and then looked at my grandmother in a 'do you understand what I am trying to say?' tone.

"So whatchu' sayin'?" she asked him, making sure she understood.

"I'm not saying anything except what I'm going to put on this police report. Renee is not here." He winked at my grandmother and she nodded.

After the officer had left, my grandmother called my Uncle Lenny. "I jes need her to stay wit you fo' a lil' while," I heard her say. "Yea. Barbara Jean acting a fool again. Okay. What time? I don't know. Yea. Umhmm. Umhmm. Yea. Okay. In a lil' bit. Okay. Bye." That was the conversation as I heard it from this side of the receiver.

††††††

Whew. My drink is starting to wear off. I want another, but my body won't move. I drifted into a deep sleep.

Chapter 3

"Nae, **where you** at?" yelled a male voice on the other side of the door. It was Kevin, knocking like he had lost his mind. I looked at the clock on the wall. It was one-thirty; in the afternoon. I got up and unlocked the door.

"Girl don't be scarin' me like that. I done been callin' you all night and monin'."

I rolled my eyes at him, ran my fingers through my hair, which I knew was all over my head, but I didn't care. I went back to the couch.

"Wus wrong withchu girl?" Kevin asked. "You look like hell."

"Kevin, what do you want?" I asked impatiently.

"Whatchu' mean what I want?" he asked. Irritation at it's worst.

"Why are you bothering me?" I yelled.

Kevin's eyes focused on the two liquor bottles that lay on the floor in front of the stereo.

"I guess that 'splains why you ain't answer the phone," he said with a sense of sarcasm.

I looked at Kevin for the first time in a long time and wondered what the hell I was thinking when I decided to go out with him; the second time. The first time was for Marlene, but after that I have no idea what it was I ever saw in him. He wasn't attractive. His pants were sagging and he had on tennis shoes. I hated when men wore tennis shoes.

Kevin was thinner that I actually preferred, and he looked like he hadn't had a hair cut in ages. I dreaded having sex with him so much that I faked orgasms just to get him off me.

He was neither soft nor affectionate. Whenever I tried to get on top and do something different, he'd immediately turn over, hump for a few minutes, grunt then turn over and fall asleep. Yippee. Actually the thought of it was quite repulsive.

To top everything that I hated about him, there was his voice. He had this country ass accent that drove me crazy. Lord knows I hated it when he opened his mouth. At times I just felt like putting tape over it. Hell, at this very moment I feel like taping up his whole body and rolling him off the balcony of my apartment.

"Renee? You hea' me tawkin' to you?" I heard him say.

"Kevin?" I said rising from the couch and walking to the door.

"What?"

"I want you to leave. And when you, please don't *ever* come back."

"Girl, you tawkin' nonsense now," he rejected.

"I'm serious as a heart attack," I told him, opening my front door waiting for him to exit.

"You still drunk ain't chu?" he asked.

I walked to the phone that hung on the wall near the kitchen. "You have thirty seconds to get your black ass out of here."

He challenged me by folding his arms across his chest and continuing to stand his ground. I raised my eyebrow at him. *Oh, he must think I'm playing with him.* I began dialing. 9..1...

"Bitch! " he yelled as he walked towards the front door. *Oh no he didn't just call me a bitch.* I put the phone on the receiver and retrieved a knife from a nearby drawer.

"What the fuck did you call me?"

He put a little pep in his step then. Actually, he started running, when I drew the knife back and aimed it right at his head. Damn. It missed him.

"You crazy bitch!" he yelled as he ran down the stairs. I slammed the door and laid back on the couch. I was feeling like shit. I buried my head in a pillow. Something has got to give. I was not a happy camper and I was starting to hate everything about myself at this particular moment. My spirituality definitely was shook.

I needed to get a new perspective on life. I knew what I wanted, but I had no drive; no direction.

"Jesus!" I said aloud. So loud, that I startled myself. I tried to get my thoughts together and figure out just what it was that I wanted to do with my life and how I was going to obtain it.

I wanted to please God. I wanted to help people that were less fortunate than me. I wanted to get married one day and have a baby. I wanted to marry a man who loved the Lord and loved me as the Bible described. I wanted a man that was ambitious and full of drive, yet affectionate and romantic. I wanted a man who knew the true meaning of "the head of household" without a needy desperation to stroke his ego or the need for him to take away my individuality. I wanted to be able to blossom into the woman that God intended for me to be.

Hell, what am I talking about, I wasn't the epitome of saved myself, however, I still knew what I wanted.

My passion is writing. I want to someday be a best selling author. I know I can give Terri McMillan a run for her money. Don't get me wrong, I love Terri's work, but I'm better. And Lord knows if Eric doesn't write something different than the typical South Cali interracial relationship, I'll scream.

I didn't decide until the last minute if I wanted my doctorate in computer science, psychology or political science. I settled on computer science, after deciding that psychology would not be the best way to go. That's funny considering how messed up I was. Imagine me telling other people what to do with their lives, when mine is in such shambles.

†††††

"Thank you Jesus," I said as I rose from my bed the next morning. I looked over at the clock that was housed by the nightstand next to my bed. It was nine o'clock. I started to call my mother, but then changed my mind instantly. Besides, she was probably getting ready for church.

I got up and stripped the sheets from my bed and threw them in the hallway onto the floor so that I could prepare to do laundry. I opened the blinds and windows. It was another sunny day in boring Colorado. One day I'm going to leave this place. After all, there wasn't one reason to stay here. I needed to go somewhere and make a life for myself.

I didn't know where I would go. I had thought about Seattle, Phoenix or Georgia. California was definitely out of the question. I had visited Los Angeles in 1992 and I hated it. I felt so claustrophobic that I couldn't wait to get home. I downed several No-Doze and made it to Denver from Los Angeles in fourteen hours. You have to be some kind of special to live in Cali. I had heard that Georgia had too many of us; black folks. Hmm. I bet Seattle is beautiful in the summertime.

I decided to take a shower before I cleaned my apartment. Shoot, I need to take my behind to church. That's where I really need to be right now. I showered, and dressed in my powder blue suit, matching blue pumps and wide brim hat. I made sure my apartment was secure and went downstairs to get in my car.

I can't believe this. Someone had busted my windshield. I could feel my face getting hot in anger. I marched back through my security gate, and knocked on my neighbor's door.

"Whattup up?" he asked. He already knew what I wanted, and at that point I knew he was going to lie.

"Can you follow me," I asked him, not waiting for him to respond. He followed me out to my car.

Once in front of my car I pointed to the crack in my windshield and said, "Who did that?"

"What?" he asked, pretending he couldn't see that big ass crack down the right side of my windshield.

"Sean who busted my window?" I asked, helping him out.

"I don't know, I haven't been here," he continued to lie.

"Stop lying Sean," I cut him off. "You got home at two o'clock this morning."

"No I didn't," he protested.

"Yes you did. And you and your little girlfriend didn't stop fighting until five-thirty this damn morning."

"I don't know how your windshield got like that." I can't stand a liar.

"Well I just want you to know, when I get back from church, I will be calling the police and I will be filing a report." He didn't say anything. He just turned around and walked back into his mother's apartment.

The funny thing about it was that I wasn't mad at the fact that my windshield was cracked. I was more pissed off at the fact that for the first year and a half that I had lived here, it was beautiful and peaceful. That was until my neighbor's two sons got out of jail and all hell broke loose. My CD player managed to come up missing from my car and now my windshield. They acted like they lived in a ghettous jungle; if ghettous is a word.

They didn't care about anything that didn't pertain to them. That's what irked me more than anything. I had been on Sean for a while to get his life together. He called himself flirting with me one day.

"You can't do anything for me out here drinking a forty ounce, cursing and kicking it with the fellas and living off your mama," I had told him.

"I betchu I could love you better than them old kats you be with," he challenged.

"I doubt it," I said bursting his bubble. I leaned in and whispered in his ear, "You see, the difference between you and those *older* kats, as you so call them, is that they are successful. They are gainfully employed and own something other than a two-hundred dollar pair of tennis shoes."

"You ain't gotta have all that to do what I could do to you," he said. I doubted his ability to even get it up with all the weed he smoked.

"Do you love the Lord Sean?" I asked him. I had no idea why I was even asking him these questions. It was a dead issue.

"All good girls love bad boys," he said.

"How do you figure that?"

"Yall do. Yall say yall want a good man, but yall don't know what one is," he said with a devilish grin on his face.

I looked at him and thought to myself, *no this punk doesn't think he has it like that.* I asked him again, "Do you love the Lord?"

"Of course I do, you know my mama is saved."

"Your mother being saved has nothing to do with *you* being saved."

"Of course I love the Lord," he finally answered.

"Oh, so when you're out here with your boys, you pour a little of your "Old E" out in the name of Jesus huh?"

"Yea, sumpthin' like that," he grinned.

"Boy get out of my face," I told him.

I debated on whether I should go ahead and go to church or go in the house and call the police. Every Sunday when I got ready to go to church, something always happened, and I always made an excuse why I couldn't go. I decided that I'd go ahead and go, and file the police report when I got back. God knows that church was where I needed to be.

✝✝✝✝✝✝

The parking lot of the church was crowded, but I managed to find a parking space on the side of the church. I walked in and purposely sat in the back, just in case I had to leave. You know, just in case the pastor saw me wanted to point me out. So much for that.

After Pastor Emery preached his sermon, he called to worship those who wanted prayer. He made his way down the isle. I hope he doesn't see me. Too late.

"Renee, do you have any sins that you want to hand over to the Lord today?" he asked. I shook my head and gave him a 'you know better' look. He continued on by.

The devil was fighting with me and I must say, he was winning. Some days I would literally pace back and forth from my bedroom to my front door trying to decide whether or not I was going to church. Some Sundays I would make it, others I wouldn't.

One Sunday after pacing back and forth, I finally made it to my car and then to church. I'll never forget that day. I wore my long red chiffon skirt and matching duster, accented with my silver stilettos, matching purse and silver hat. I knew I was looking good. Well at least until I fell down the stairs that led to the sanctuary. The devil had managed to possess me once more. I wanted to get up and flee from the church, never to return.

Just as I was turning to leave, Sister Diana opened the prayer room and walked into the sanctuary. She looked at me and smiled. I changed my mind and walked into the sanctuary behind her. That was my confirmation that I had done the right thing by going.

†††††††

*A*fter church, I came home and called the police. The only thing the officer did was take a report and give me a case number.

"Is that all you guys do?" I asked the officer.

"Unfortunately yes. You didn't actually witness the crime, so there's not much we can do about it. You can give your insurance company this case number." So much for my insurance rates.

I took off my suit and put on some sweats and a tank top and continued with my cleaning. I wiped down the walls with ammonia, poured bleach into the shower stall in my bathroom and the tub in the main bathroom. I cleaned mirrors, sinks, toilets and mopped floors. I did the laundry, cleaned the kitchen and dusted and polished the furniture.

When I was done vacuuming, I sprinkled Glade's Lilac Spring carpet freshener throughout my condo and sprayed air freshener of the same scent through the air. I lit the Lilac Spring candles I had placed strategically around the apartment. My place smelled so good, I could smell it at the bottom of the steps when I went to empty the trash. The phone rang as I walked up the stairs.

"Hello?" I answered.

"I'm surprised you at home. But then again it *is* Sunday. I don't suppose nobody would find you in a church house no way."
This woman just got out of church and she had nothing better to do than to call and work my nerves. I tried to stay calm. I couldn't let my mother get to me no matter how much she wanted to.

"Praise the Lord to you too Mama. As a matter of fact, I just got back from church." I wasn't giving her a chance to go in for the kill.

"Now that is shocking. I guess the Lord *can* work miracles."

"And yet on your way to Hometown Buffet, you found it spiritually necessary to give me a phone call eh?"

"Don't get smart with me heffa," she said. Like she intended, she was working my last nerve. I needed her to hurry up and get off my phone.

"Do you need to go to the store today?" I asked her.

"It *would* be nice," she said sarcastically.

"I'm on my way," I said hanging up the phone, before she could get another word out edgewise.

I wiped my body down with some Summer's Eve wipes and changed into a Fila t-shirt and headed to my mother's home in North Denver.

When I pulled in front of her apartment, I noticed that she had her door open. She had company. Her friend Maxine. Great, she's going to visit all day and expect me to wait for her.

"Are you ready?" I asked when I walked in the door.

"You can't speak?" she asked in an effort to embarrass me.

"Hello Maxine," I said reverting my attention to my mother's company.

"How have you been Renee?" she responded. "I swear you done got prettier and look more and more like your Mama."

"Thank you," I said trying to act flattered. Little did she know, I hardly considered it a compliment. I could hear my mother suck her teeth. I looked at her and caught her rolling her eyes.

I heard a male voice coming from the spare bedroom. I knew it was Eddie talking on the phone. I also knew that if Eddie was using the phone, he had to be living with my mother. When it came to Eddie, my mother was always hush hush about everything. I know she didn't call me all the way over here to take her to the store and he was here.

I turned to my mother and asked her again, " Are you ready?"

"Can't you see I have company?" she snapped. I was so sick of this shit.

I turned to Maxine and said, "It was nice seeing you again Maxine." I walked towards the door and said to my mother, "Call me when you're ready. Or better yet, let Eddie take you to the store." I sucked my teeth not looking at her as I walked out the door.

"Where do you think your going'?" I heard her say behind me. She had put her proper demeanor on. I kept walking, got into my car and drove off. Yet again, my mother managed to ruin my entire day.

I drove away wondering to myself why I came in the first place. Why did I continue to allow my mother to do this to me? The truth is that in some way I hoped that my mother would eventually wake up and start loving me like a mother is supposed to love her daughter and somehow complete me. I shook that notion when my cell phone rang.

"Hello?" I asked without looking at my caller ID.

"Why do you always have to be such a disappointment?" my mother yelled on the other side of the phone. I clicked the power button on my cell phone just in time to prevent myself from hitting the car in front of me.

"Dammit! She makes me so mad. I hate her! I hate her!" I yelled as I hit the steering wheel.

When my exit came up, I decided to keep straight and get off at Peoria Street. I wondered what Marlene was up to.
I turned my cell phone back on. The message alert yodeled Yankee Doodle. I dialed Marlene's number. She answered on the first ring, panting hysterically.

"What?" she said, knocking the base of the phone on the floor.

"Why don't you answer the phone just like every other human being?"

"Renee, what do you want?" she asked abruptly.

"Excuse you?" I came back.

"I thought you were someone else."

"If you had caller ID you wouldn't have this problem." I said.

"I'm busy," she said coldly and hung up the receiver. *No she didn't,* I thought. I was infuriated as I got back on the highway and headed home.

Once in front of my garage, I shut off the engine and sat for a moment. A tear escaped my eye. Something had to change, and it had to change fast. I tried to think of something that would bring me joy. The only thing that I could think of was my career and Charlie. Working as a stock broker at Charles Schwab took my mind off most of my problems. I realized that throwing myself into my career only covered the underlying problems and when I left the office, they were right around the corner waiting for me.

Charlie Thatcher was my best friend and we shared a common bond; our belief in love. Although he worked at our home office in San Francisco, Charlie and I had daily contact. It was nothing for Charlie to jump on a plane at my beck and call and fly out to Denver to spend time with me. He had proven there was nothing that he would not do for me. Occasionally, I would feel guilty from time to time, because all I had to offer Charlie was my friendship. He would remind me that, my friendship was all the required.

Once again Yankee Doodle rang from my cell phone. I checked my messages; five. Two were from Kevin, one from my mother, one from Charlie and one from Stuart Humphries. I immediately deleted the messages from Kevin and my mother. I didn't want to hear what either had to say.

"Hello Luv. I'm starting to think you don't love me anymore. Call me soon. Chow for now." That was Charlie. I hit the number two key on the dial pad on my phone and saved his message.

"Stuart Humphries. Stuart Humphries," I said to myself. Why did that name sound familiar? I listened to the message.

"Hey sweetie. Long time no chat. Give me a call at 619-555-3136, or you can call my cell at 619-555-2246. I look forward to hearing from you. Oh and Renee, I miss you."

My curiosity had the best of me now. Why was Stuart, of all people, calling me? Stuart lived in San Diego and I had met him over the Internet. Actually I had known Stuart via the Internet for three years and although I had plenty of pictures, I had never met him in person.

"I'm not calling this fool," I told myself.

††††††

I **could hear** my answering machine beep when I got to the door or my condo. Once inside, I turned off my phone and pulled down the blinds. I reached into the cabinet and retrieved a bottle of wine from the fridge and sat down in front of the television. The answering machine was still beeping. I ignored it. I began switching channels on the television until I stopped at "Titanic". I was a sucker for romantic movies. You know how the story goes. Boy meets girl, boy charms girl; girl falls in love and they lived happily ever after. In this case, boy meets girl, they fall in love, boy dies putting girls life ahead of his own. How sad; yet romantic. I put my head in my hands and laugh to myself. Who makes this shit up? I began to cry.

The answering machine beeped again. I looked at the caller ID. My mother, Charlie, Kevin and Kevin's mother. I knew I had better call Charlie because if I didn't soon he would be knocking on my front door in worry.

"You know I was just finishing packing. You were about to force me to come to see if something happened to you," Charlie said when he answered the phone.

"I'm sorry sweetie. I've been so stressed out lately that I haven't been up for much conversation lately."

"Conversation? Is that what I am to you now?" Why did I have to say it like that and why did he have to take it so personal?

"You know what I mean."

"Are you seeing someone? Is that it? If so, then I can kind of understand. Otherwise, there should be no reason that you feel that you can't pick up the phone and call me. For anything."

"I know Charlie. But you know me. Sometimes, I just don't want to bother others with my issues."

Silence. Something told me that something was bothering Charlie. I decided to take the attention *and* the heat from myself and direct it to him.

"Hey you. What's wrong? Sounds like it's more than my not calling you back."

"Just worried about you is all."

"Hmmm. You're getting too upset just to be worried about me."

"Luv?"

"Umhmm?"

"I miss you."

"I miss you too Charlie. Stop trying to change the subject."

"I'm not. I really miss you." I wondered where he was going with this.

"What's going on Charlie? Are you okay? Are your parents okay?"

Silence. I knew at that point that something had to be wrong with one of his parents.

"Charlie? Is there something wrong with Fred and Marie?"

"Dad's in the hospital." He had my attention now. I stood up from the couch and paced back and forth in front of it.

"What happened? Is he okay? Are you Okay? Is Marie with him?" I had a million questions.

"He had a heart attack," Charlie answered.

"Why, how, when?"

"The doctor tells me that Dad's been sick for a while and he knew it. Mom knew it, but they both failed to tell me."

"I'm sure they didn't want to worry you," I tried to comfort him.

"They had to know I'd find out. They just had to."

"Is Marie with him now?"

"Yes," he sulked.

"Why aren't you with him Charlie?"

"Because he said he doesn't want me to come. I protested, but he refuses. Something about living my life to its fullest. But I think that he is embarrassed because he didn't tell me. I can't believe mom didn't tell me."

I can. Marie was a selfish racist bitch. Nothing she did or didn't do surprised me one bit.

"I'm sure she had her reasons," I told him. I would never tell Charlie that I despised his mother. "So how are things looking now? Is he going to recover?"

"They've moved him from ICU and he's in a regular room, but it scared the hell out of me Nae. You know?"

I wish that I was with Charlie. I could tell he needed a hug and someone to lean on right now.

"Charlie do you want me to come down and help out. You know, be there for you?"

"I'd give anything to be with you right now, but I don't want you to come down just yet. I think I really need to get away."

"Is that a good idea with your dad being bed ridden?"

"Probably not," he said. I could tell he was disappointed at my suggestion. I was really at a loss for words. I didn't know what to say. I don't know how I would react if I was told my mother had a heart attack and could die should she have another one. "Hold on, my other line is ringing," Charlie said.

I held on and twiddled with my hair clip.

"Luv, it's the hospital. I'm going to have to take this," Charlie said when he switched back over.

"Okay, keep me up to date on what's going on. You stay strong. Remember if you need me I'm here."

"I know. I love you Nae."

"I love you too Charlie."

I thought against unplugging the answering machine. I didn't want to miss Charlie's call. I popped " The Brothers" into my DVD player. I watched it at least once a week, and I was about due for my Morris Chestnut fix.

It amazed me how I never got sick of watching this movie. The underlying message in the movie was about overcoming past hurts and allowing yourself to love and be loved. I think if it weren't for my admiration of Morris Chestnut and a few other select black men, I would have given completely up on the black man.

Just as Jackson was feeding Denise the last piece of wedding cake my cell phone rang. I looked at the LCD display. Much to my disappointment it was not Charlie. The name was unavailable but the number was 619-555-3136. It was Stuart. At first I wasn't going to answer it, but curiosity once again got the best of me.

"Hello?" I said in the sultriest voice I could muster up.

"Hey sweetheart," he said.

"Who is this?" I asked.

"You forgot about me that quick," he asked chuckling.

"Who is this?" I asked again this time firmly.

"It's Stuart,"

"Stuart who?" He chuckled, sighed, and then paused.

"I believe you have the wrong number," I said.

"Wait. It's Stuart Humphries from San Diego, you know, Mr. True Gent."

"Oh," I said trying to act totally surprised. "How are you?"

"I can't believe you forgot about me that quick."

"Well it *has* been a while since we last chatted."

"I must not have left a lasting impression. That's damaging to my ego you know?"

"Well If I remember correctly, you have enough ego to last a lifetime" I joked.

"Umph. You're still feisty. Just like I remembered," he said.

"So err Stuart to what do I owe this call to?" I asked getting to the point.

"Actually I've been working on a new brokerage project and I was elected to help launch it at the Technology Fair down there in DTC."

"Techno Expo?" I asked. He had my attention now. I had represented Schwab in the Expo every year for the last four years.

"Yes. So you *do* keep up on current events," he said. I took a hard swallow.

"Yes, I will be demonstrating our new Online Brokerage rollout."

"What a coincidence," he said with mischief in his voice.

"That's the 18-22nd right?" I asked.

"That's right. This is great because I was hoping that while I was down there, we could hook up."

"Hook up?" I asked with attitude.

"You know what I mean," he responded apologetic.

"No I don't know what you mean."

"I apologize, I said that wrong," he said trying to repair the damage he had just caused. "What I meant was, I would love to finally meet the lady that has intrigued me for so long. Maybe have dinner, do a little dancing and indulge in some stimulating conversation."

I hung up the phone and thought to myself, *no this fool didn't think he was going to come down here for a booty call.* I looked over at the television and realized that the screen was blue.

Chapter 4

The **next morning**, I got into the office early. I wanted to make sure everything was on schedule for the Expo. I had planned a long day of contacting clients and trying to promote our new product.

"Markets up 300," Ken said as I got off the elevator and headed towards my office. Ken worked in foreign markets and always greeted me at my office with a cup of coffee, just the way I liked it; hot, black, sweet and with a touch of cream. Rumor had it that Ken was sweet on me, but I didn't believe it. I actually thought Ken was a little sweet himself.

"Blue chips?" I asked.

"Kickin' ass," he replied.

"Leaders?"

"Gates announced a two for one; Gerstner announced above average earnings."

"Lows?"

"Sun Micro, underestimated earrings and possible lay-offs."

"FUTSI?"

"Closed."

I looked at Ken, "Holiday?" I asked.

"Yes Ma'am," he replied.

"Have I ever told you that you were the greatest?"

"Every day." We smiled at each other.

I sat down at my computer and checked my email. Thirty-three; mostly internal. My eye focused on one titled: Itinerary. It was from MrTruGent@aol.com.

"Goodness he never gives up," I said aloud.

"Who?" Ken asked.

"Oh nothing," I said brushing him off.

"Renee?"

"Yes?" I asked not looking up from my email. I was curious as to what it said. I opened it. I could hear Ken in the background, but I didn't hear a word he said. I read the e-mail.

Surprise! It's me. I just wanted to send you a copy of my itinerary while I'm in town. I also wanted to apologize if I came off the wrong way. It was certainly not my intention to do so. I hope you will reconsider the dinner proposal. Well, see ya in a few weeks.
                                        Always, Stuart.

"Hello!" I heard Ken yodel. I had almost forgotten that he was in the room.

"Oh I'm sorry, what did you say?"

"Never mind," he said, getting up to leave.

"Sit down Ken. I apologize," I said trying to make him feel better. "You have my undivided attention." He looked at me for a minute, gazing into my eyes and not blinking.

"I asked you what you thought of interracial relationships," he repeated.

"Well, Ken, I hadn't really given it much thought, but I believe that love has no color. Why do you ask?"

"Well there's this woman. I'm attracted to her and I really want to approach her. But the problem is, I don't know how or even if I should."

"Have you thought about just coming out and telling her you feel?" I asked.

"No," he said. "I wouldn't even know how to start."

"Well maybe you should take a deep breath and understand that the worse thing she can say is she is not interested. It won't be the end of the world. You'll never know until you do. *She'll* never know until you do. You know, the direct approach is always the best approach?"

The phone on my desk rang. I pressed the speaker button. "Yes Joanna?"

"Miss Matthews, Charlie Thatcher is on line two ," said my assistant.

"Put him through." I waited for my partner in crime to speak.

"Renee?"

"Charlie, how the heck are you?" I asked gleefully.

"Doing good. Did you get my message?."

"When did you leave it?"

"I've left you a couple of messages last night and one this morning. I called to give you an update on dad's condition."

"I'm sorry Charlie. I don't know why I didn't get them. I don't know why I didn't hear my phone ring. I waited for you to call last night and eventually fell asleep on the couch. But I still should have gotten your call."

"Check your messages later," he said. I could tell he was agitated and it was almost as if he was crying. I don't recall the phone ringing while I was on the phone with Stuart but I could have missed it. I felt really bad.

"Charlie? Fred's okay right?" The more Charlie remained silent, the more I was worried. "Charlie?"

"Yeah," he managed to say.

"I'm so glad to hear that. How is Marie doing?"

Ken, feeling neglected, motioned me with his index finger that he'd come back another time. I waved to him as he disappeared behind the closed door.

"As good to be as expected I guess. I think I am taking it harder than she is."

"I'm going to clear my calendar and head out there. You don't need to be by yourself right now."

"No Renee. Dad didn't want a funeral. So he'll be cremated."

"Charlie, I want to be there for you," I pleaded.

"You are. Just know that you are. Hey, how is the tech project coming along?" I wanted to push the issue with Charlie, but thought against it.

"Almost wrapped up. Did you get that assistant for me?" I asked him.

"Yes, he's going to flying out a few days before the expo. I've set up a meeting for you two to get acquainted and go over details before set up."

"Do you have my itinerary?" I asked Charlie.

"You should have it. I sent it to you on Saturday."

"Hold on," I said, checking my e-mail. "Okay, got it. Let me see." I scanned the itinerary, something about it looked familiar, but I couldn't figure out why.

"Okay Charlie, this looks good. What's the 411 on my assistant?"

"Oh yeah that info is attached. Use word to open it." I open the word doc file and my mouth dropped wide open.

"Charlie?"

"Yeah?"

"Who picked my assistant and where did he come from?"

"Janet at headquarters referred him. Said she's used him before and he did such a great job. He came highly recommended, and I figured since our turn out last year wasn't all it could have been, it would be a great idea." I couldn't believe it.

He continued, "I've talked to him via video conference, and I gotta tell ya Nae, the guy has character. He's bound to get consumers to our booth."

"He's got character alright," I mumbled.

"What was that?" he asked.

"Oh nothing. Just thinking out loud." I didn't want to seem petty, however, something down inside me knew that Stuart knew before he called me that he would be assisting me at the Tech Expo.

"Chuck, is Mr. Humphries on our payroll?" I asked out of curiosity.

"No, not yet. Right now he's independent, although, Janet says she has his resume on file. If the

Expo goes well, we'll be making him an offer. Are the arrangements to your liking? I'm sensing a little hesitation."

"No, Charlie, everything is fine. I'm just making sure that I have all my Is dotted and Ts crossed. Looks like everything is ready to go."

"Okay Renee, oh and I also need a sample presentation packet."

"That went out to you Friday, via Fed Ex, so you should be getting that today."

"That's what I love about you Renee, always on the top of things."

"Thanks Charlie, it helps when you love what you do and love your colleagues just as much."

"Kiss up," he chuckled.

"You bet your ass," I joked back hanging up the line.

I sat in my office for a moment and looked out the window. I glanced across the highway at the mountain scenery and business buildings behind it. I wished that I could wipe away Charlie's pain. I knew there was something that he wasn't telling me. I dialed the number to the San Francisco Veterans Affairs Medical Hospital. While I waited to be connected to Fred's room, I wondered what exactly it was that Stuart was up to.

"Third floor nursing station, Simone speaking."

"Yes, my name is Renee Thatcher. I'm trying to find out how my father in law Fred Thatcher is doing." Okay, so I lied.

"I'm sorry Mrs. Thatcher, I assumed that everyone in the family was notified."

I felt a sharp pain in the pit of my stomach and everything that I had eaten that day acted as if it wanted to come back up.

"Mrs. Thatcher?" the nurse said.

"Yes. Yes I'm here. What is happening to my father in law?"

"Mrs. Thatcher, your father in law passed last night. Again, I was under the impression that everyone was notified."

"I was out of town and was only told to get back as soon as possible."

"I'm sorry you had to find out this way. Have you not talked to your husband?" she asked.

"I did, but he said he could not tell me over the phone and to get home quick. I have not seen him since I returned home a few hours ago."

"I see," she said.

"Thank you. Simone is it?"

"Yes."

"Thank you Simone."

"You're very welcome Mrs. Thatcher." I hung up the phone and felt like such a selfish fool. At the same time I was so angry with Charlie for not telling me. I guess had I not been on the phone lollygagging with Stuart, I would not have missed Charlie's call.

I hit the speed dial button to Charlie's office. He didn't answer. I hit the speed dial button to his cell phone.

"Did I forget something?" he answered.

"Yes, you did."

"What?"

"Why didn't you tell me Fred passed away?"

"I tried. You weren't there. Or rather you didn't answer when I called last night."

"Charlie, I told you I don't know how I missed your call. You've talked to me twice today and both times you failed to tell me."

Beep.

"Miss Matthews, your mother is on line three, do you want me to pass the call?" Joanna asked.

I sighed, "Thank you Joanna. Yes. Put her through."

"Hello Mother," I said uneasily.

"Praises Renee," she replied. I rolled my eyes into the back of my head and mustered up enough strength to speak to her.

"How are you feeling today Mother?"

"I'm blessed Renee," she said sarcastically. She didn't say anything after that.

I broke the silence, "Did you need anything?"

"I been sittin' here for two days with no food Renee, what tha' hell you think I need?"

"Whose fault is that Mama?" I asked her.

"I called you all weekend to come.." she began, but I cut her off.

"Mama," I said. She had managed to piss me off. "I came by twice to take you to the store and you found something else better to do. My scheduled does not include jumping at your every beck and call. I do have a life you know. Besides I know Eddie is living with you. Why do you have a grown ass man living with you and you have no food? I bet you Eddie eats. He's in good health. Why do you feel the need to call me from clear across town to take you to the store, when one, you're capable of driving and two, Eddie is capable of driving. I know I couldn't get away with that."

"You a selfish heffa Renee. Lord only knows why I didn't abort you when Memah told me to." My head began to throb.

My mother had told me that she had called back home to Longview when she found out she was pregnant, asking her if she could come back home. My grandmother told her only if she aborted the baby. I never asked my grandmother the real reason because I knew she would never tell me the truth.

"So why didn't you mother? Why do you always bring up what you could have done, or what you should have done? I'm here now and I'm a grown ass woman, and there isn't a damn thing you can do about it." I grabbed a tissue from the nearby box and dabbed my face to stop the tears from ruining my make-up.

"Now I'm going to ask you again, is there anything important you called me for?" I asked trying another approach.

"Ain't you heard a damn thing I said!" she yelled. This was the last straw.

"All these brothers and sisters you have in this town, dammit, have one of them do whatever you need. Hell, have Eddie do it. I don't care. I'm a grown woman, and I will no longer allow you to disrespect me." I hung up the phone. I held my head in my hands and tried to calm down. For as far as I could remember my mother was always a cruel woman.

I had almost given up my faith in God because growing up, we spent four out of seven days in church. My mother was a deaconess, and always praised the Lord and yelled and screamed hallelujah on the inside of church, but as soon as we got outside, she was cursing, or being hateful or mean. If that was what God was about, I wanted no part of it.

I needed to get some more coffee. I walked outside my office and stopped at Joanna's desk.

"Good morning Joanna.

"Good Morning Miss Matthews."

"Do you have anything for me?"

"Yes. I have three messages. One was from Charlie, and you've already talked to him so I discarded that one. The second one is from Janet in headquarters and the third one was you're your mother. She just called again, but after that last conversation, I didn't think you were ready to talk to her."

"You heard me all the way out here?" I asked embarrassed.

"Yes, but I wasn't eavesdropping," she added in defense.

"Oh sweetie, I know that. I just didn't realize I was being loud. Thanks for letting me know." Joanna had been my assistant for three years now and I had always been able to count on her.

"You did good," I assured her. She finally smiled.

"Oh I forgot, this came for you this morning," she handed me an overnight envelope. It was from headquarters.

"Thank you Joanna," I said as I walked back into my office. I sat down at my desk and opened the package. It was a proposal letter. I was being offered a promotion in San Diego. I looked the documents over. The position was Analyst Director of U.S. markets. The pay was nearly triple that of what I was earning now. What in the world would I do in San Diego? I didn't know anyone there. Stuart. This was all becoming too eerie for me. I pressed the speaker button on my phone and hit the speed dial button for Charlie.

"Chuck speaking" he answered.

"It's me," I announced. He chuckled.

"You mean you knew about this?"

"Well that depends on what you're talking about," he said still chuckling.

"The proposal."

"Yes, isn't it great? Someone in headquarters must love your work Renee. So have you decided what you're going to do?" he asked excited for me.

"No, I just got it like five minutes ago. What the hell am I going to do in San Diego? I don't know anyone in San Diego. I don't even like California."

Charlie broke out in a loud hysteria. I didn't see anything the least bit funny.

"What's so funny?" I asked.

"You've only been to L.A. Foreigners always associate the entire state of California with Los Angeles. Trust me, San Diego, is much different."

"I don't know Charlie," I said with hesitation.

"Look at it this way. You get the chance to experience a new environment, a new culture and enjoy the beautiful weather that San Diego has to offer. And you can come up to Frisco and visit me."

"How far is Frisco from Diego?" I asked him.

"About ten hours I think, but the flight is about an hour or two."

"You know I hate flying."

"Well we're going to have to work on that aren't we?"

"What about what I have established here?"

"Renee, c'mon. You can't be serious Luv. What exactly have you established here? Do you own a home? No. You have no children, no husband. And God knows you need distance from you mother." He paused for a minute. "I'm sorry. I shouldn't have said that."

"Oh no, you're right about that. I do need to get away from her before she drives me crazy."

"There, you said it. What else or who else could possibly be holding you here but you?" Charlie had a point. There was really nothing holding me here. There were no attachments.

"But California's so expensive," I tried another approach.

"Ree?"

"What?"

"Since when have you had to worry about money? All the green you make, you could afford to take care of myself and a few of the Five Points homeless."

I laughed. "Well I'm going to think about it. I should have a definite answer by early next week."

"Renee, think long and hard. This could be a chance of a lifetime for you. Do you want me to fly out and spend some time with you."

"No, you don't have to do that, although, I wouldn't mind the company." I paused for a moment. "You know, why don't you come," I said changing my mind,

"But after this Tech Expo. Right now, I don't need any distractions."

"Okay, that is fine. If you are going to make me wait, I'll wait."

"Charlie, what would I do without you?" I knew Charlie had no intentions of waiting. I knew that he had probably already made flight arrangements to Denver.

"Not a damn thing my dear, not a damn thing." The accent in his voice made me smile.

††††††

After **work** I went home and ordered Chinese. I did not feel up to cooking. I checked my answering machine. No Messages. I found that pretty odd. I checked the cords on my machine. They seemed to be working properly. I jumped when the phone rang. I thought surely I would have a heart attack.

"Hello."

"Girl, you too busy to hang witcha' girl huh?" It was Marlene.

"Seemed like the last time we spoke you were a little too busy."

"Oh girl, stop trippin'. Michael was over and we was getting our groove on." I didn't say anything.

After a moments silence, she said, "So What's up with you?"

"Work," was all I said.

"So when we gone hang out?" she asked.

"I don't know. I have the tech expo to do. That has been taking up most of my time. I'll sure be glad when it's over.

"I hear ya. Hey Renee? I was wondering if you could loan me fifteen hundred dollars."

"Fifteen?' I yelped. "I just gave you eight hundred two weeks ago."

"I know. I'm still waiting for this gig."

"Why do you need fifteen-hundred," I asked suspiciously.

"To pay a few bills and get a few things."

"I thought your parents were paying your bills Marlene."

"Can I borrow the money or not Renee?" she asked.

"You can come get it tomorrow. I'm not bringing it to you."

After I hung up the phone, it realized that San Diego sounded more of a possibility than not. I looked around my condo, and thought about past times. I had been in this very same place for the last four years. A new place excited me, yet scared me. A million questions ran through my mind along with fantasies of endless possibilities.

†††††

It **was seven** o'clock when I decided to go to the gym. I headed to 24 Hour Fitness. It wasn't as crowded as usual.

"Yes!" I heard a male voice say when I was on the leg press machine. I turned to the familiar voice to find myself staring at one of the most attractive men I had ever seen. He was watching the NBA finals on a nearby television. I knew instantly who he was.

"It's a wrap," I said and continued my workout.

"Laker fan?" he asked failing to turn to see who he was talking to.

"You had to ask?" I came back.

"Well, yes. Now if you were a Nugget fan, then I could understand, but Denver doesn't have an over abundance of Laker fans."

"Guess that makes me special doesn't it." I said. He finally turned and looked in my direction. He chuckled and put his head down.

"Ohhh, a sassy Laker fan at that. I like that."

"Hello Mr. Humphries," I nodded in his direction.

"Ms. Renee Matthews." He studied me from head to toe. Give me a break. He walked to where I was and leaned in for a hug.

"Unh, Unh. You're funky," I joked extending my hand to him. He actually appeared to be offended. I gave him a non-challant gaze and walked to the seated row machine. I saw him from the corner of my eye still standing in the same spot where I had left him. He was still watching me. I did my reps and left the gym.

††††††

*A*gain, when I got home, I could hear my answering machine beep before I opened the door. I just knew at least one had to be Stuart. Much to my surprise and disappointment, there was only one and it was from my mother.

2:45p.m. "Nae this is your mother. Did you forget my phone number?" Click. It dawned on me that I hadn't told my mother my decision to move to San Diego.

"Hello Mother. How are you today."

"Blessed," was all she said.

"Did you need something?" I asked after a few seconds.

"Do I have to need something for my daughter to call to see if I'm alive."

"Well, you only call me when you need something."

"Well, I need some things moved to storage and I just bought a new sofa table I need you to help me with that and I need to go to the store." Here we go again.

"Well let me take a shower and then I'll be over."

"Renee don't take all day!" she yelled.

"I said I'll be over as soon as I take a shower. I have to talk to you anyway."

"About what this time?" she asked. "I sure hope it ain't one of those mother-daughter talks, 'cause I ain't in the mood."

I hung up. It was at that very moment that I decided I would be taking the position in San Diego. If there was any skepticism about me staying, there was not an inkling of it now.

When I arrived at my mother's apartment, the door was open as usual. When I went in, I didn't see her and concluded that she was in the bathroom. I didn't see Eddie either. I saw the table in question and removed it from the box. I scanned her living room and wondered how she was able to fit anything else in her small apartment. The small empty space by her Queen Anne chair was the only place I could imagine she wanted it, so I set it up next to it.

After I was done, Eddie walked through the door.

"Sup big sis."

"Hey Eddie," I acknowledge him.

"Whatchu' up to?"

"Trying to figure out why Mama is calling me getting on my damn nerves when you live here."

"Whatchu' mean?" he asked. The closer he got to me, I could tell that he had been smoking weed.

"She has been calling me almost every day telling me that she needs to go to the store because she didn't have any food."

"You know she lyin'."

"And why did she call me all the way over here to put together this table and you could have done it?"

"I dunno. That's yalls drama."

I watched him walk into the kitchen and open the fridge and retrieve a Miller Beer. He was right. The fridge was full of food. I should have known better.

"How do you know I wanted that there?" I heard my mother ask behind me. I looked at Eddie who was now sitting at the kitchen table.

"I didn't. I assumed since this was the only logical place it would fit, you would want it here."

"Tha's yo' problem, you always assuming. I didn't tell you to put it there."

"Where do you want it Mama?" I asked, already knowing that was exactly where she wanted it.

"Just leave it there."

"Mama, we need to talk."

"Renee, I told you I ain't up for one of your mother and daughter talks."

"Why not mama?" I was getting irritated by the minute. "Why are we having difficulty having a successful relationship?"

"Renee, I did the best I could with you. I don't owe you nothin'. I did what the law said I had to. I clothed, fed and sheltered you. Like you said, you a grown ass woman now. I don't owe you nothin' else."

I looked at her and for once felt sorry for her. If I ever got married, she would miss out on the love of grandchildren. I looked at Eddie once more. He shrugged his shoulders.

"Do you need anything else Mama?" I asked her.

"Whenever I needed you, you seemed to be too busy, so I do what I have to do my damn self."

"Good mama," I said. "Get used to it."

"I don't know why I even bother with you Renee?"

" You know what Mama?" I said, getting up to leave. "I don't either. And you won't have to anymore." She had moved me beyond my boiling point.

I turned to my brother and said, "By the way Eddie,I'm moving to San Diego. I want you to come and visit me when I get settled in."

"For real?" he sounded excited for me. "When you leavin'?"

"As soon as I possibly can."

"Why you leavin'?"

"Because there is no reason to stay here,"I said, shutting the door behind me. I wanted to go to San Diego now more than ever and I never wanted to see my mother again. I heard the door open behind me.

"What the hell do you mean you're moving to San Diego? When? And when were you going to tell me?" my mother yelled.

"I just told you," I shouted.

"I'll be damned.   I should have aborted your ass when I had the chance!" she shouted.

"That doesn't hurt me anymore Mama. You can say it till you're blue in the face. You didn't abort me. I'm here dammit, and I'm glad. I thank you for not aborting me. Because I'm going to show the world that I will never be like you. That is my number one goal, to never ever be like you." I got in my car and drove away. It wouldn't move me if I never saw her again.

Chapter 5

I **decided to** turn into the K-mart parking lot on Chambers Road and Colfax and get some toiletries. My cell phone rang.

"Luv?"

"Hey Charlie," I said gleefully. I was happy to hear his voice.

"What are you up to, Luv?"

"In K-mart, getting some personal items."

"I see," he said.

"Well?"

"Well what?" I asked, already knowing what he was waiting for.

"You're killing me here Ree."

"You act as if you have some vested interest in me coming to California."

"I do," he said.

"Is that right. And what might that interest be."

"Why do you have to know everything? Stop trying to be in control all the time."

"Now I know you don't want to go there with me sweetie. Do you?"

"No I don't. But I would like to know what you decided."

I sighed, "Call the movers Charlie."

"Yes!" he said in excitement, accidentally dropping the phone.

"Ouch. I'm going to be deaf before I get there."

"I am so happy you decided to take the offer. You have no idea how happy this makes me."

I was starting to feel like he was more excited about my move than I was.

"What are you doing?" I asked Charlie, longing for his presence.

"Cooking your dinner."

"No way," I said.

"Way."

"Where are you?"

"At your place," he said. I knew Charlie would ignore my wishes for him to wait until after the Techno Expo.

"I'll be there in an hour," I told him and hung up the phone. I honestly don't know what I would do without Charlie. He was my support system, my shoulder to lean on and my friend when I was in need. No matter what I did, wrong or right, Charlie was there for me. Although I had feelings for Charlie, I suppressed those feelings and acted dumbfounded when he tried to express his. I felt things were better that way. My issue with Charlie was not Charlie himself, it was his mother I had a problem with. Charlie's father adored me. His mother was another story.

"You're getting to close to that negro woman," I heard her say to him from the kitchen, one day when Charlie invited me to his parents for dinner.

"Don't mind her," Mr. Thatcher had said. "She would find something wrong with you if you were a honky too." His comment took me by surprise, but yet made me feel a little at ease.

Yep," he said, relaxing his folded hands on his crossed knee. "Our son adores you, and that's all that matters to me. I mean God didn't see color right?"

"No he didn't." I still wasn't completely comfortable. "No he didn't," I said again, but much lower.

††††††

*W*hen **I got** back to my condo, the aroma of Italian food had attacked my nose. I looked around the kitchen and gawked at the mess Charlie had made.

"I hope you don't mind Luv,"

"No not at all. Because I know that you know that I know that you know that I know that you are going to clean up that mess right?" I asked giving him a playful tap.

"I just knew when you said an hour, you meant two hours," we both chuckled. "I thought I'd have it clean before you got here." Charlie took a loaf of bread from the stove.

"Is that fresh bread?" I asked.

"From scratch."

I pinched a piece from the side. It tasted like heaven. "Mmmm," I said. I looked in the corner of the hallway.

"Charlie how long have you *really* been here?"

"Hmmm. A couple of hours." His eyes followed mine to the packed boxes.

"I figured, I might as well help you get a move on."

"You didn't have to do that Charlie, you know that."

"I know that I don't have to do anything I don't want to Luv. I do it because I want to." He kissed me on the forehead.

"So did you shop up an appetite?"

"You know I did."

"Well let me fix you a plate and you can show me all the things you bought and we can start making plans for your move to San Diego."

Charlie and I spent the next few hours eating. He actually laughed at my new dress I picked up from Foleys.

"Looks kind of homely," he teased.

"Where are your things?" I asked.

"They're in the car. I'm going to check into Embassy Suites later."

"Why in the world would you go to a hotel Charlie," I said irritated.

"Because the last time I slept on your couch, I fell off from all of the tossing and turning."

"Whose fault was it that you slept on the couch?"

"Mine. But.."

"You don't have to sleep on the couch," I interrupted him. The red wine was starting to get the best of me. "It is possible for us to sleep in the same bed and still be platonic ya know?"

"I know. But I didn't want to make you feel uncomfortable in any kind of way."

I grabbed Charlie by the hand. "Let's go to bed," I said flirting. I was feeling sexy and aroused from all the wine I had consumed. Charlie stood like a tree stump, standing his ground.

"Ahhh I see. My little cupcake has had too much to drink. I'm going to put you to bed and I'm going to sleep on the couch."

I unbuttoned my blouse revealing my red lace bra. I walked over to Charlie, put my hands on his waist and looked up at him.

"Kiss me," I said.

"Ree, I'm not going to allow you to do something that you will regret in the morning."

"Is that to say that you'll regret it?" I asked.

"No way in hell. But this is not about me. This is about you."

"I want you, Charlie," I said.

"No you don't. It's the alcohol talking."

I unbuckled his belt not taking my eyes off his. His face turned beet red.

"You'd deny me pleasure?" I asked knowing I was working him thin.

"Ree, it's no secret that I love you and that I want you too. But I'm not about to jeopardize the respect and love we have between each other for a roll in the sack.

"Charlie, anybody ever tell you that you talk to much?" I asked.

"All the time," he chuckled.

"Oh well, I guess I'll go to bed alone. And touch myself," I said putting a great deal of emphasis on *touch myself.* I turned around, and slowly walked to my bedroom, letting my blouse drop to the floor revealing my red lace bra that I had purchased from Frederick's of Hollywood. Before I got the entrance of my bedroom, I seductively relieved myself of the skirt I was wearing and let it fall to the floor, exposing matching red lace thongs, and sashayed into the bedroom. That did the trick because before I knew it Charlie was behind me, cupping my breasts and lightly biting my neck.

"Tell me you won't hate me in the morning," he said with a tremble in his voice.

"I won't hate you in the morning," I whispered. "I'll love you some more in the morning; and some more and some more." That was all the reassurance that Charlie needed. He turned me around picked me up, straddled my legs around his waist and put my back against the wall.

Charlie had more passion than I expected from a white man. He started at my forehead and planted soft, seductive kisses on my face, before sucking on my lips. I was surprised and refreshed at the same time. All the black men I had been with were less considerate, less passionate and only wanted to get right to it. Needless to say, each time I was left unfulfilled.

"You have no idea how I feel right now," he said, hot breath blowing in my face, making my nipples harder.

"I have an idea," I said, reaching down and touching his manhood. His tongue entered my mouth, first with hesitation, then I realized that he was teasing me. I was burning with desire for Charlie. He began to bite softly on my neck as I held my head back with pleasure running my fingers through his thick salt and pepper hair.

"You are so beautiful," he whispered. "And so sexy."

I massaged his shoulders and whispered "Take me to the tub." Charlie secured me around his waist and walking into the master bathroom.

I put bubble bath in the tub and turned on the faucet. As the water and the bubbles rose, so did my desire for Charlie. I sat on his lap, grinding my groin against his, kissing him passionately with my tongue. I figured that the myth about white men having small penises was not at all true when I felt his bulge tickle my fancy. Once the tub was full, I turned off the faucet.

"You sit right here, and don't move," I told him. I stepped into the pool of bubbles and disappeared until only my head was showing. Charlie lit the candles that I had placed strategically around the bathroom.

"Turn on the stereo," I said. I watch Charlie as he turned on the Bose CD system that sat neatly on the shelf above the toilet. Light jazz music filled the air.

I've been here before. I mean, I've looked at Charlie with desiring eyes before, but each time I did it was as if I saw something new. I watched the way Charlie moved with such smoothness and finesse. His tall, muscular frame was very well taken care of and he had impeccable hygiene habits. Charlie turned to me and did a few of his salsa moves as he made his way back to the tub. Umph, Umph, Umph! *There has got to be a brotha in there somewhere*.

"What are you smiling at?" he asked catching my gaze.

"You," I said.

"Like what you see?"

"Yes Indeedy." Whew! I turned away from him. If it was possible for a black woman to blush, I was doing a whole heck of a lot of it right now. I emerged from the water as the candlelight glistened on my sudsy silhouette.

"Okay Charlie. We are going to play a little game. I touch a part of my body and you tell me when I get to a spot you that you like."

"I like all your spots," he said, as serious as the sky is blue.

"Work with me here." I ran my hands through my hair, never taking my eyes from his. I could see desire dance in his eyes. He wanted me and I wanted him. I ran my fingertips lightly across my facial features; my forehead, my eyes, which I closed for a brief moment, re-opening them as I touched my nose. I touched my cheeks, outlining my lips slowly, stopping to suck the length of my index finger into my mouth.

I traced my shoulder with my fingertips and began to massage my breasts, stopping at my nipples. I could see Charlie's tenseness. I outlined the dark line that ran down the middle of my torso stopping at the top of my pubic area. With a raised leg resting on the side of the tub, I bent to caress my toes, exposing a silver toe ring, up to my thighs. I traced the insides all the while looking at him. I turned around and bent over to retrieve the sponge from the bath water.

Charlie's manhood began to take notice as it bulged against his jeans. With my back to him, I stood up and squeezed the sponge over my back as the suds slowly rode the contours of my buttocks. I turned around and stared him. The sparkle in his eyes was tantalizing.

This was too much for Charlie to bear. He removed his shirt and with jeans still intact, got into the bathtub with me. He took my face into his hands and began to taste my lips. I was caught off guard. But feeling too aroused, I surrendered, kissing him back. Charlie kissed every inch of my body, from my head to my feet. He kneeled down in front of me, raising my right leg to rest on his shoulder. He tasted my sweetness, as I moaned in pleasure running my fingers through his hair and massaging his shoulders. I loved the way his tongue tickled my fancy.

"Charlie make love to me," I whispered in weakness.

"What was that?" he asked.

"Make love to me." I repeated. Charlie picked me up, stepped out of the bathtub and carried me to the bedroom. He laid my naked body onto the bed, kneeled down and tasted me some more.

"Make love to me," I said again.

Charlie stood up and removed his drenched jeans and briefs. He slowly entered me as we both moaned in pleasure.

I rolled him onto his back and straddled myself on top of him. I slowly thrust my hips up and down as I saw the pleasure in Charlie's eyes.

"I love you," he said. "More than life itself."

"I love you too," I returned. Damn. It was too late. I had already said it. Although I was sincere and meant it, I didn't want to say it; not to him. But now I couldn't take it back now. That night, the love we made, the love we shared, was the best I had ever had.

††††††

The next morning I was awakened by the smell of scrambled eggs. I opened my eyes and stared at the ceiling. I wondered if the pervious night had happened or was I only dreaming. The scent of the night before engulfed my body. I had to take a shower. Charlie had set out some Victoria' Secret Dream Angels, body wash, lotion and cologne on the brass shelf that lined the tub. A sponge, a large bath towel and a purple terry cloth robe sat next to it. Charlie was one of the most considerate men I knew.

I looked at the boxes that Charlie had packed the day before and took a deep sigh. Butterflies began to dance in the pit of my stomach. Soon, this would no longer be a place that I would call home. Wow. San Diego. Never in a million years would I have thought I'd be a Cali girl. This was all becoming so overwhelming.

After a quick shower I walked into the kitchen. There stood Charlie, standing over the stove cooking what appeared to be an omelet.

"Good morning Luv," he said. "You look great naked." I had not put anything on after my shower and had totally disregarded the purple robe he had laid out for me.

"Thank you," I cracked a fake smile. "Umm. Charlie, we need to talk."

"You hungry?" he asked ignoring my request.

"Charlie?"

"Let me ask you something Ree," he said.

"Go ahead."

"I told you that I loved you last night. That I love you. You told me the same. Did you mean it?" He was standing in front of me with hurt in his eyes. Hurting him was the last thing I wanted to do, but he had to understand my reasoning. I loved him, but it wasn't that easy.

"Yes I meant it, but things are so complicated," I said.

"Complicated? How?" he asked. I had his full attention now.

"You're my best friend."

"That's the beauty of it. We have a bond. We trust each other. We know each other's faults. We accept the other for who they are and we don't try to change that. Best friends make the best lovers," he defended.

"Yes, but then there are the other issues?"

He put crossed his arms over his chest. "You mean like my being white right?"

"Truthfully, yes."

"It doesn't bother me that you're black. Hell I don't see a color when I look at you. All I see is beauty. Why should it bother you that I'm white," he asked. "Are you saying that when you look at me that you see me as a white man? When you told me you loved me last night, did you see me as a white man?" He was now standing in front of me, holding my face in his hands.

"It doesn't bother me that you're white. It's just that..."

"When we made love to each other last night, did my color bother you? Were you worried about who thought what about our relationship?"

"No," I answered. This was exactly why I had refrained from revealing my feelings to Charlie. I felt so bad. I was sure this would put a wedge in our relationship and possibly ruin our friendship.

"Neither did I," he said picking me up and placing me on the island in the middle of the kitchen. A moment of awkward silence between us as he looked deep into my eyes as if he was trying to search my soul for the truth; I with tears slowly escaping my eyes.

"Ree, we've known each other too long for us to be at this point. I gather you feel the same about me that I do about you. I know that. But something else is holding you back. I need to know what it is. We need to talk about it and find a solution."

I kept my mouth close, because I felt at this point, nothing I said would soften the blow or ease the pain that Charlie was currently feeling.

"I can deal with being your friend. Really I can. What I *can't* deal with, is knowing that we adore each other and we have these feelings for each other. I *can't* deal with knowing that we are destined to be together and something is keeping us apart. *That* Luv, is something I can't deal with." He turned to walk away.

"Charlie." I didn't know what to say, but I didn't want him to leave. I didn't want him to walk away. I didn't want to hurt him. I wanted him to understand why I felt the way I did. Only I didn't know how to tell him, or if I did, if he would even understand.

"Charlie," I called to him again. When he turned around his face was a bright shade of red and his eyes were bloodshot red from the burning of the tears that he was unsuccessful in holding back.

"If you want me to leave, I will. I'll be back when you're ready to head to San Diego."

"I don't want you to leave. I just want you to understand." By now we both were both having a full fledged bawl out.

"Help me understand Ree. You love me but you can't be with me?"

"I told you, it's more complicated than that."

"What's more complicated? We're talking about love here. There are no such things as complications where love is concerned." He walked back towards me. "We've always talked about wanting someone to love. Real love. We have that Ree. What complications?" The pitch of his voice got higher. He raised his hands to his forehead.

I had seen Charlie emotional before, even upset, but he had never been this upset with me. I gave him an apologetic look.

"Are you hungry?" he asked. This was Charlie's way of saying, let it go for now.

"Not much of an appetite right now."

"I didn't mean to upset you. Just a little frustrated is all."

"I know. It's my fault."

"It's no one's fault. It's just the way things are sometimes."

"Eat just a little. For me? Please?" Charlie's omelets *did* smell good and he could make one hell of an omelet. Everything Charlie cooked was awesome.

Charlie fed me little bites and took some for himself in the process. We ate in silence. Just our facial expressions and eye contact doing the communication for us. As he fed me, I thought back to a conversation that Charlie and I had before I met his parents. He had told me that I was the only woman that could keep a smile on his face. I was the only woman that made him feel young and silly. I was the only woman that he would give everything up for. I smiled at that memory. Hmph.

"What?" he asked.

"Nothing. Just taking a trip back down memory lane."

"I hope that's a good thing," he said.

"Yes, most definitely."

"Well, are you going to share?"

"No," was all I said, my smile as wide as the Grand Canyon. He kissed me on my forehead and looked into my eyes.

"Okay, Okay. I know better than to argue with you."

Charlie must have seen the longing in my eyes. They had to reveal the desire I had for him. My eyes must have given away my need to be with him, because he started breathing heavy in my face. Self-control had been thrown out the window long ago.

"I'm scared," I whispered, breathing as equally as hard as he. For what happened next, I could have kicked myself.

I played with the hair on his chest. Neither of us could hold back what we felt at that moment. He kneaded my breast and he softly kissed in between them. I ran my hands along his shoulders messaging them then running them along the length of his masculine arms. He began to circle one of my nipples with the tip of his tongue as if he was teasing an ice cream cone that he was preparing to devour. I let out a soft moan as I continuously ran my hands along his. Charlie repeated the act on my other breast.

Our lips met as Charlie's tongue penetrated my warm and wet mouth. He kissed my chin, and ran his tongue from the tip of it, down my neck, in between my breasts down my stomach and stopped at my belly button. I massaged his head, firmly pushing it down to my now heated desire. Charlie devoured me as if God had ordered all females to be banished from the earth forever. I arched my head back and moaned still massaging Charlie's head. I lifted my legs to give him easier access to my garden of forbidden fruit.

"Yessssss. Mmmm. Yes," I softly moaned.

After fifteen minutes, Charlie came up for air and found himself exploring my warm mouth again.

"I want to taste you, I told him. I slid off of the island and kneeled down in front of Charlie. I took his strong manhood into the palm of my hands and began to message it. I heard him let out a moan. I cupped his desire with my left hand as I ran my hand up and down his shaft with the other. I devoured him like a Tootsie Pop and I was trying to get to its creamy center.

"Fuck me," I told him. "I want you." All sensibility went out the door. Charlie picked me up and secured me around his waist. He walked over to the kitchen table, knocking everything on it to the floor. He pulled me to the edge of the table. I welcomed Charlie's male being and slowly slid down on it. More moaning.

"Yes, Luv," Charlie said. "My darling, you are everything to me."

"This is all for you." I told him. Charlie massaged my breast, running an occasional finger over my throat as I arched my neck. He touched my pubic hair and massaged my warm spot. We both arrived at the same time. Damn. I had just made a complicated issue *more* complicated.

I **turned back** to look at the empty condo that I had called home for so many years. The silence let out a loud echo. I had spent most of my memorable moments, right here in this living room. I had several secret rendezvous' here. I remembered the ones with Gerald Levert, Johnny Gill, Carl Thomas and Kevon Edmonds. Oh and then there were the ones I spent with Earth, Wind and Fire, as we sipped White Zinfandel and Moscoto together.

I had spent several days and nights here with Karl Malone, Shaquille O'Neal, Kobe Bryant, Rick Fox and Robert Horry, cheering them on as loud as my lungs would allow.

I had cried and looked admiringly in the eyes of Morris Chestnut, Bruce Willis, Sean Connery and Tavis Smiley. I closed my eyes, took a deep breath, said goodbye, and closed the door behind me. I had decided that I would push my move forward and fly back for the Techno Expo. I was to spend a couple of days with Charlie in San Francisco. My things wouldn't arrive for a few days.

A limo was waiting outside to sweep us off to the airport. Saying goodbye to my life in Colorado was one of the hardest things I've ever had to do. I lay my head in Charlie's chest the entire ride to the airport; in silence.

I gazed around the airport once we reached the gate at Denver International before boarding the American Airlines flight to San Francisco. I don't know why I had never come out here before to see the new airport. After Stapleton was shut down and this airport was built, I told myself it was too far to drive. Part of me wished I had visited it just once. But none of that really made a difference now. I took a deep breath and sighed.

Charlie squeezed my hand. "You're going to be all right Luv." That was Charlie's specialty, making everything all right. If he only knew of the demons that plagued my head, plagued my past and prevented me from giving him the love he deserved. God knows I wanted to give it to him, but he would never be able to understand or even accept me if he did.

My cell phone rang. The caller ID read *Mom*. I didn't want to talk to her until I got settled into San Diego, and at this moment, I didn't care if I ever spoke to her again.

"Ma'am, you will need to turn off your cell phone until we land in San Francisco."

"I'm sorry, I forgot to turn it off," I apologized to the flight attendant, as I turned off the phone. After take off, the flight attendant asked if I wanted anything to drink.

"Do you have Moscoto?" I asked, knowing there was a slim chance that she did.

"I'm sorry, we have Chardonnay, Merlot, Zinfandel...."

"I'll take Zinfandel, thank you," I interrupted her.

"And you sir?"

"I'll have a diet coke," Charlie said.

"Diet coke?" I said looking at him. "Since when do you drink diet Coke?"

"Since I fell in love," he said smiling at me.

Although I enjoyed the passion I had shared with Charlie, I wish it had never happened. I wanted it to happen. It shouldn't have, but I couldn't take it back. I was more confused now than I was before that night. I didn't want to lose him as a friend, but I knew I had put our friendship in jeopardy. Neither of us had any idea where we would go from here. I guess we would have to just wait and see.

I sipped on the glass of wine the flight attendant had brought to me and laid my head back to relax. I had no idea what lie ahead of me. A new start, a new career, a new state, a new life. An entirely new world was about to open up for me. I tried to think of all the things I would miss in Colorado. The only conclusion I came to were my co-workers at the firm.

I felt somewhat guilty when the thought of not missing my mother screamed in my head. I would no longer have to endure her cruelty, selfishness and control. I certainly wouldn't miss Marlene. I mailed her a check for the fifteen hundred dollars she had asked to borrow, not expecting to get it back. I simply wrote a note: *Just consider this a good-bye gift from me to you.*

My mind wandered back to my mother. Although, I felt as if I was being freed from an emotional prison, the truth of the matter was that my mother was my lifeline. She is what kept me going. When she told me I couldn't do something, I did it. I didn't realize it until this very moment that it was her negativity that gave me the drive and ambition that I had. Could I make it without her?

"Maybe this is a mistake," I said. Charlie looked in my direction without looking at me and raised his eyebrow.

"We can turn around and go back if you'd like. But as your friend, I would strongly advise against it."

"Charlie I don't know if I can do this?" I was starting to doubt myself and fear was becoming a large factor in my rational.

"Ree, what's so different?"

I tried to think of every excuse, but the more I thought of one, it sounded more foolish than the one before. Charlie had never shown anger towards me, even when I had hurt him, but I could tell that at this moment he was becoming quite irritated.

"You were trapped in Denver. You wouldn't allow yourself to develop and grow," Charlie began to preach. "By God you're so used to being controlled by your mother, you don't know what you want."

I sighed. Part of me wanted to get angry with him and ask him who gave him the right to evaluate my life, but the other part knew that he was right. I had to grow up. And I would; eventually.

I realized, growing up in Colorado, that it was not the place for a black person, especially not for someone looking to be successful. Colorado was segregated, with the exception of the few interracial couples in the middle-income and poor neighborhoods. Surviving racism was an every day task for me.

I can remember years ago when Lord & Taylor opened their store in Cherry Creek; a posh upper-middle class, predominately white neighborhood. It was the talk of the town. The store was featured on the local news channels and in the local papers. Denver was surely setting its position on the "major city" map.

I dressed up and went to the grand opening. From the time I walked in the front door until the time I walked out, security was on my tail. I browsed the shoe and the purse section. I became very irritated when an older white salesperson made it her business to inform me of the price of each item I looked at.

"That is a thirty-five hundred dollar purse. If you can afford that, we have shoes that will go great with that."

"No thank you, I'm just looking for a new purse," I responded. I knew I didn't belong in this store. I couldn't afford anything in here. Well at least if I wanted to continue to have a place to stay, because I definitely would be using my rent money.

"That purse is a little cheaper, it's seven hundred dollars," she said after I had zoned in on another selection. My sole purpose of being here was to see what all the buzz was about.

I ended up leaving with a purse that cost two hundred and seventy-five dollars, and a red suit that cost three hundred and ninety-five dollars. I smirked at the sales woman as I exited the store. The look on her face reeked pure anger.

Needless to say, I waited until the next day and returned the items I had bought the day before. I didn't have to put myself at a disadvantage to prove a point to a racist. I thank God that I was now in a position to walk into that very same store today and buy whatever I wanted with no problems.

Trying to gain respect at work was a long uphill battle. If I didn't get the racial jokes, got my share of sexual ones. And although I held one of the top positions at my firm, I knew that California would take me where I really wanted to go. I knew that my new experiences would allow me to grow a little and experience things that I had only dreamed of.

††††††

I had dozed off, only to be awakened by the pilot's voice over the loud speaker. Charlie had fallen asleep on my shoulder.

"Please fasten your seatbelts. We will be landing in beautiful San Francisco, in just a few minutes. We at American Airlines would like to thank you for flying with us and enjoy your stay in San Francisco."

I looked out the window and exposed myself to the most beautiful skyline I had ever seen. The skyline of the San Francisco International Airport was bordered by water and landscape that looked like architectural drawings from the plane's window. The stick like figures formed into people, as we got closer to land. I was as amazed as a child on their first of many bouts to Disneyland.

"This is amazing," I said aloud.

"Sure is," Charlie had awakened.

"How was your nap?" I asked him.

"Short."

I had a smile bigger than the Rocky Mountains. As we walked through the gate to the airport, I wondered why I was so surprised when I saw and entourage holding a big sign that said *Welcome to California Renee*. When Charlie did something, he went all out. The sign was being propped by two people. One I didn't know, the other I did. It was Derrick from Smith Barney, better referred to by Schwabites as Smarney. Both of us worked there some years ago.

"Welcome to California Luv," Charlie said giving me a tight hug.

"You sure know how to make a girl feel at home don't you?"

"Only the best for my darling."

I shook the hand of the unfamiliar woman who held the welcome banner and introduced myself.

"Hello, I'm Renee."

"Hello Renee, I'm Ramona. Charlie has talked about you non-stop for as long as I can remember."

"All good I hope," I said nudging Charlie in the side.

"Nothing but." Ramona was a middle-aged woman of evident mixed descent. Forty-four is what I would have guessed. A further guess would have made her of African-American and Hispanic descent. She stood a few inches taller than myself sporting long beautiful curly auburn hair. Even at this age, she could probably give Jennifer Lopez a run for her money.

I reverted my attention to Derrick. "Nice to see you again," I said, turning back to Charlie. The last thing I really wanted to do was engage in an informal conversation with Derrick.

Derrick and I didn't see eye to eye. He didn't like me and I didn't like him. I couldn't quite put my hand on exactly why we didn't like one another, but I'm willing to bet that it dates back to when I declined his invitation to go out on a date with him. I had gone out with Victor instead; a white man.

"How do you two know each other?" I asked Charlie.

"I stole him from Smarney. He is going to give you guys a hand on the Expo project." I gave Charlie a blank stare. I had almost forgot that I had to return to Denver once more to pull off the expo. Charlie gave me an unexpected kiss on the forehead and put his arm around my waist as he scurried me to baggage claim area.

"Are you ready, Luv?" he asked.

"Yes, I am."

"I figured we'd stay in Frisco for a couple of days then we could drive down to San Diego, and get you situated. Schwab had given me a thirty-day leave in order to make my transition just as long as I agreed to come back for the Expo.

"Just relax and enjoy yourself," he told me. Of course after we had claimed our luggage, a limo waited for us curbside. I asked Charlie to let down his window so that I could get a clearer view of San Francisco. The buildings reminded me of ancient Rome.

"All of this looks so frightening."

"Darn tourist," Derrick mumbled.

"You've never been here?" Ramona asked me.

"Nope," was all I said. I didn't even look at Derrick even though I wanted to shoot him an evil look.

"Charlie this is so beautiful," I said kissing him on his cheek. I could feel Derrick's gaze burn the side of my face. I was sure he was not pleased with my admiration for Charlie. I never understood for the life of me, why black men found it necessary to proudly flaunt white women but got steaming mad when a black woman did the same. I pretended not to notice.

San Francisco was nothing like I had imagined. Although it wasn't my taste, it was different, and it was new. I remained silent for a few miles, watching the scenery go by. I was in total awe when we pulled up to a nice three-story home at the top of a hill. The driveway curved around to the front door, passing the three-car garage. This had to be Charlie's home. I couldn't imagine why he worked with the firm, with all the money he had.

"It keeps me busy and out of trouble," he had once said.

"Not too shabby," I said trying to act non-amused. Charlie didn't speak. He just smiled at me. The driver came to my door first and let me out.

"Madam," he said, extending his hand. I got out and admired the tan stucco home. The driveway was a tan marble with specs of gold and silver. There were windows everywhere. I waited for Charlie where I stood. He walked around the limo and took my hand as he led me to the front door. He put the key into the lock.

"Charlie.." I began.

"Shhh," was all he said. We entered the immaculate home, and I was amazed at Charlie's good taste. I looked around, wanting to speak, knowing if I did, Charlie would only order me to be quiet.

"Luv, I have to make a phone call, why don't you pick out a bottle of wine from the cellar," he said in his English accent.

"Where *is* the cellar?" I asked.

"I'm sure you'll find it, Luv. I really need to make this call."

I was irritated at his sudden urgency to use the phone. I eventually found the cellar, which was off the kitchen, which was off what appeared to be the family room. The kitchen's décor was stainless steel complimented by marble counter tops. An island inhabited the middle of the kitchen. It housed a range.

I opened both doors of the cellar and found a bottle of wine. I couldn't decide from the many types that Charlie had to choose from. I finally settled on a bottle of 1998 Cabaret Sauvignon. I turned around to find Charlie leaned against the doorway smiling.

"Ok," he said rubbing his hands together, "I just got off the phone with the realtor in San Diego and your place is ready. We just need to go down and inspect it and make sure it's to your liking."

"Realtor?" I exclaimed. "What would I need a realtor for?"

"You're even sexy when you attempt to play dumb Luv," he said. I gave him a puzzled look.

"I think these are for you," Derrick said, passing me an envelope. I opened the envelope not even giving him a glance. They were papers to a house located at 12056 Sandy Sail Lane, Coronado, CA, 92118.

"These are in my name," I said. I should have known Charlie was up to no good.

"Yep," was all he said. I looked at the specifications on the inspection sheet. 4200 square feet, bi-level, cul-de-sac, five-bedroom, four and half baths, family room, game room, large eat in kitchen with detached dining room, living room, sun room, office/nook, three-car garage, rooftop deck. The list went on and on. I couldn't believe Charlie had gone and done this. More complications. I was starting to feel that he wasn't making an attempt to respect my feelings. I dark cloud appeared over my head briefly until I noticed the signature date on the papers. It was signed only weeks before. My mouth fell open.

"I think you better grab her Charlie before she falls out, she's not looking so well right now." that was Ramona. I had almost forgotten she was with us. She was so quiet.

The papers were in my name *only*. It showed that a down payment was made of $350,000.

"Charlie, I can't accept this. Why would you do something like this? You know how I feel about..." he interrupted me.

"Keep your socks on Luv. I know how strong and bullheaded you are. You don't have to sign it if you don't want to."

"I don't understand," I said, still not understanding why I was holding paperwork in my hand to a house that belonged to me that I had not earned.

"Goodness," Derrick mumbled as he walked out to the limo and leaned against the back of it. He was really working my nerve, but I refused to show it.

"Are we going to stand here all night and dispute this my Luv? Just think about it." I had seen that look in Charlie's eye before. It was the same look that I saw in his eyes when we had the argument in my apartment back in Denver, and one time before when I had told him that we had to re-evaluate our relationship and "just be friends".

I looked at Ramona who looked back at me and said, "You deserve it." Ramona didn't know me from a slice of bread, how she figured I deserved this, I had no idea.

"You okay Luv?" Charlie asked, chewing gum. I could tell he was the one aggravated now.

"I just want to be alone right now," I told him. Charlie had the limo driver take Derrick and Ramona wherever it was they had to go, and then joined me in the living room.

"Charlie, why would you do something like this," I asked him.

"Why wouldn't I? Look Ree, when someone loves you, there is nothing they won't do for you."

"But we aren't together," I intercepted. Charlie swallowed hard. I didn't mean it the way it sounded, but I'm sure he took it that way.

"Ree, we don't have to be together, for me to love you. Besides, like you said, our friendship is worth more than anything right?" His hurt shone through. I reached out for him, but he walked out of the living room. I plopped down on the couch and sighed. Tears escaped my eyes, first slowly, then in a steady stream.

When Charlie came back into the living room, his face was as red as his eyes were. He got on his knees in front of me.

"Look Ree. I will say this to you always. I love you. And you mean the world to me. Now, I don't regret what happened back in Denver. I loved every moment of it. I wanted it to happen. I've wanted it to happen for years. I want it to happen again and I'm not going to apologize for that." He made me feel so vulnerable. I listened, knowing I wanted it to happen just as much as he did.

"If it never happens again," he continued, "That will be just fine with me. All I want is your complete happiness, and if that is not with me, then whomever. But I will always be honest with you about how I feel. And, dammit, if I feel like showering you with gifts of appreciation, then I will. All you have to do is say no." He stood up and walked away. I could hear him mumble, "I have all this gotdamn money and no one to share it with. What good is it?"

I was starting to see the stern side of Charlie more than ever. It was actually turning me on. But I knew I had to keep my cool. Another episode like the one in Denver, and I knew there would be no turning back. I had to be careful with every move I made; I was in unknown territory.

"Promise me, that you will always be in my life, no matter what form that is," Charlie said, walking back into the room. He began pacing.

"I promise Charlie."

"Are you hungry?" he asked changing the subject.

"Famished," I said. He looked at me and shook his head.

"What'd I do now?"

"Famished?" he chuckled. "Alrighty then. Let's go for a drive and a bite to eat."

Charlie showed me the sights of San Francisco. We ate at Farallon's in Frisco's Union Square.

"You'll love it here. I know how you like seafood," Charlie said after we entered the restaurant.

After dinner, we retreated back to Charlie's for a glass of wine. "You can have the master suite, Luv, and I'll sleep in one of the spare rooms."

"We can sleep in the same bed, yanno?" I said wondering why the hell I had said it after it was too late to keep my mouth shut. Damn. I talk too much.

"You know what happened last time."

"I think we can sleep in the same bed and not make love."

"Ya think? You are pretty irresistible. I'll make you a deal. You don't sleep in any of that sexy lingerie that we both love so much and we will be fine."

I laughed, "But that is all I have."

"I think I have some sweats and a t-shirt in the closet in there." Charlie and I held each other, talked and eventually fell asleep. We made it through the night; without having sex.

††††††

The next morning we showered and decided to head down to San Diego. The drive was breathtaking and exhilarating. I had never seen such beauty. Well, except on television, but something was different about seeing it all in person. The closest I had gotten to nature was taking in the Aspen trees in the Rocky Mountains. Truth be told, I'll take sandy waters over autumn leaves any day.

"The ocean, is so beautiful and serene," I commented.

"Yes it is. Get used to it. San Diego is especially beautiful."

Nine hours later, after dozing off several times, I looked around to see where we were. I saw that we were on Interstate 5 as we approached a sign that said *San*

Diego 29 miles. I fell instantly in love. I took in the aura of the fresh water smell, and wondered why I had ever doubted making the move in the first place.

Shortly after leaving Carlsbad, Charlie said, "That's the place I told you about. You know the one. Where you can pick your own fresh strawberries."

"Ah, I'd love to do that one day," I said, ecstatic. There were times that no matter how much I tried to act experienced, my naïveté shone through. This was one of those times. Here I was experiencing a world that I had no idea existed and I was acting like a child in a candy store.

"That right there on your right is the Del Mar Fairgrounds," he pointed. "Every year horses race there, and it is also the home of the world famous Del Mar Fair."

A few miles up the road we were merging from the Interstate 805 onto Interstate 8 West. "And this, my Luv, is Mission Valley."

"*Ahhh* the infamous Mission Valley," I said. "So what part of San Diego am I going to be living in again?"

"Coronado. It's a little island off San Diego. About twenty minutes from where we are now."

"Cool," with great enthusiasm. About fifteen minutes later we were driving over the Coronado Bridge. I held my stomach.

"You okay over there?"

"Yes. It's just that I'm afraid of heights and I can't swim. This feels a little eerie."

"We'll be off in a few."

"Isn't this a famous bridge?"

"Yes, would you like to hear the history behind this very bridge?"

"Sure," I said. Another thing I admired about Charlie was that he was very knowledgeable and intelligent.

"Well, it was built around 1969," he started.

"That's when I was born," I mumbled.

"Wow, I thought you were young. I guess I will have to trade you in for a newer model." I rolled my eyes at him.

"It's a little over two miles long and nearly seventy thousand cars drive through this bridge on a daily basis," he continued.

"I bet they make a killing on that toll."

"Yeppers. Let me show you the beach before we go look at your new place." It was awesome, the sunset against the most beautiful shade of Indigo water I had ever seen; another confirmation that I would love it here.

"This is so fantastic," I said to myself forgetting that Charlie even existed. "Amazing."

"I thought you might like this."

"Like it? I love it."

"Well let's get over to your place before it gets too late so we can check in at the Hotel Del Coronado."

"Sounds fancy."

"It is." A few minutes later we pulled up into a curved drive that led up a small hill to the front of a humungous house.

"This can't be it?" I asked, my eyes nearly popping out of my head. From the outside, the house was bigger than Charlie's. I looked back and forth from Charlie and the house.

The rooftop deck that faced the view of the ocean was the first thing to catch my attention. The exterior of the house was of gray stone. The front door consisted of two wooden French doors, and like Charlie's home, had windows galore. A large palm tree was housed in the front yard of plush green grass. The two-story home was one of only three houses on that particular block.

"I could have some flowers planted in front if you'd like. You know, to kind of give it that homey look."

"Oh no, you've done way too much as it is," I interjected.

"We've already had this conversation," Charlie mumbled. I tried to lighten the mood by playfully spanking Charlie on his buttocks.

"Don't be getting smart with me." Before I knew it, Charlie had whisked me off of my feet, pretended to kick in the front door and take me over the threshold.

"You're a friggin' hoot, Charlie," I said.

"Friggin' hoot?" he asked. "Now that doesn't sound right coming from your mouth, Luv." He paused for a moment before saying, "You're not turning white on me are you?" We both laughed. Charlie gave me a tour of my new house, stopping in each room to inspect every square foot.

"You act like you've been here before," I said.

"I have. I wanted to make sure everything was perfect. There were some things that needed to be changed, and by the looks of it, they have been fixed."

I put my hand around Charlie's arm. "Charlie?"

"Yes, Luv?"

"You know, everything doesn't have to be perfect."

"For you it does," he responded.

"No, it doesn't," I said looking into his eyes. "It's okay not to be perfect all the time." Charlie bent down and gave me the softest kiss. I felt weak and rubbery. I took a deep breath, parted myself from his company and explored the rest of the house.

"Luv, do you have the itinerary for the Expo?" I heard Charlie shout from upstairs.

"Yes, hold on a second," I said retrieving my purse from the kitchen counter. I figured I had better set my phone on the charger and check my messages. I hadn't checked them since I left Denver.

"Here you go sweetie," I said handing Charlie the itinerary, nearly out of breath from climbing the staircase. " I'm going to check my messages. I'm sure I have a zillion of them." Sure enough, I had twenty-one messages. There were three from my mother. Only three. Hmmm.

That was rather shocking. As usual she had nothing good to say to me. In her third message, she actually said she hated me and wished I was never born, and that she would never forgive me for leaving her in Denver; alone. *Get over it*, I puffed.

There were ten messages from Marlene expressing her dissatisfaction for my dropping her the way I did. In one of her messages she said that Kevin was looking for me. Oh well. He certainly won't be finding me here.

Much to my surprise there were two messages from Kevin and one from his mother. Basically she said that her son was devastated after our break-up and wanted to know if there was any chance that we could get back together.

"God can change any situation," she said in her message. *God won't be changing this one*, I thought to myself. There was a message from the real estate broker and a message from the movers giving an anticipated date on when my things would arrive. The last two messages were from Stuart.

"Hello Renee, its Stuart. Wanted to see if we needed to do any further preparations for the Tech Expo. Give me a call so we can discuss this further."

The second message. "Look I was thinking, before I head back to San Diego, I would like to take you out to dinner. What do you think? Give me a call." He had no idea I was in San Diego, and I wanted to keep it that way for as long as possible.

    I **walked into** the Charles Schwab office after returning back to Denver. "Renee!" Joanna screamed excited to see me.

"You have no idea how missed you are around here."

"You guys don't miss me. I bet you all had a party as soon as I left," I joked. Joanna made her way around her desk and greeted me with a hug.

"Has Stuart arrived yet?" I asked.

"Yes. He's been here a few days now. He's in your office. I mean your old office," Joanne giggled.

"What's so funny?" I asked her.

"He's a hottie," she whispered.

I rolled my eyes at her, "Oh brother. Girl you are crazy."

I walked into my old office and found Stuart looking at the Tech Expo banner. His back was facing the door. Nice butt, I thought. I stared at his physique for a few seconds. I would have put Stuart at six feet, three inches. His medium build had a nice cut. I could tell even through his dress shirt, that he kept in shape and was at the gym regularly.

"Looks nice," I finally said. Stuart turned around in surprise.

"Why thank you," he said in all his arrogance. His smile was enough to melt butter.

"I meant the banner," I said rolling my eyes. I couldn't stand an arrogant man, and Stuart was an arrogant man.

"I know what you meant," he said, knowing that I was really talking about him. I walked over to the window.

"I sure miss this office."

"Miss?" Stuart said. I guess he was going find out sooner or later.

"Yes. I live in San Diego now." His mouth flew open and seemed to stick in that position for a few moments.

"Wow," I'm speechless

"That's a first," I mumbled.

"I wondered where all your paraphernalia was. When did all this happen?"

"About a week ago," I said.

"Wow," he repeated. "And you weren't going to tell me?" he said appearing to be offended.

"I didn't feel obligated."

"I mean, well, I just..."

"I didn't think there was a need to tell you." I was firmer this time.

"Hard woman you are."

"Anyway," I said, trying not to get into a spat with the person I had to spend the next three days with.

"All the media material is ready. I went down to the Convention Center to check out the proximity of our space."

"Seems like we have everything in order."

"Oh, I forgot one thing," I said dialing Joanna's extension. Stuart looked at me puzzled but didn't say a word. "Joanna? Can you confirm Derrick's itinerary for me please dear."

"Yes Miss Matthews. His flight arrives at five-thirty." I looked at my watch. It was twelve fifteen. I had some time to kill before I was to pick Derrick up from the airport. God knows I did not want to pick him up. Just my luck, I had to spend the next couple of days with "Arrogant and Arroganter". Just my friggin' luck.

"Are you staying at your mother's or at a hotel?" Stuart asked me. I had almost forgot my mother existed.

"I'll be staying at a hotel."

"Which one?" he asked with a devilish grin on his face.

"Hotel ala none of your damn business," I told him.

"Fiesty. Umph. Umph. Umph." His gaze met with mine, and I could have sworn he undressed me with his eyes. "How about you meeting me half way and join me for lunch. We can pick up Derrick together."

"No thank you," I said looking at the great job the printers had done on the pamphlets. But then again, if Stuart *was* with me when I picked up Derrick, I wouldn't have to engage in any unnecessary conversation with either of them.

"On second thought, what did you have in mind?"

"I was thinking about Racine's," he said.

"Isn't that downtown?"

"I think so. You know more about the area than I do."

"Hmmmm. I'm trying to decide. You know, I think you might like Benihana's," I suggested.

"Okay. I can do Benihana's. I've been there a few times."

"There's a Benihana in San Diego?" I asked.

"There sure is," he said in his usual cocky tone. I frowned at him and sucked my teeth. He just chuckled.

"So what part of San Diego will you be living in?" he asked trying to break the monotony.

"Coronado," I replied.

"Coronado?" he asked surprised. "Nice area. Nice taste. They must be paying you the big bucks for you to be able to afford a house in Coronado," he said.

"They pay me pretty decent," I said. "My home was only nine-fifty." He choked on the water that he had just squeezed into his mouth from the Deja Blue water bottle.

"You mean your rent is nine hundred and fifty dollars?"

"No," I said snidely. "I mean my mortgage is nine hundred and fifty thousand dollars."

"Damn!" he said. I looked at him with my own sense of superciliousness. I was not about to tell him that Charlie purchased the house for me. No one needed to know that.

"Well let's go eat. I'm hungry."

"Whose fault is that?" he asked.

"Mine, I suppose." On the way out of the office, I stopped by Joanna's desk.

"Joanna, were going to be at Benihana's in Tamarac. From there we're going to pick Derrick up from DIA. You still have my cell number right?"

"Yes Miss Matthews."

"Call me Renee please. I've been meaning to tell you that for the last couple of years." We both laughed.

††††††

It was two o'clock before we got to Benihana's. I was always fascinated at the way the chefs sliced and diced your food right in front of you. I watched in amazement.

"I've always loved this place," Stuart said.

"Me too," I agreed. I ordered sushi and Stuart ordered steak.

"You eat sushi?" Stuart asked with a sense of surprise in his voice.

"Yes," I answered sarcastically. "Why do you seem so surprised?"

"Black folks don't eat sushi," he said.

"Well I'm not black folk," I said flatly. "What does race have to do with what I eat anyway?" I asked.

"Nothing. It's just that most black folks don't eat sushi. I bet you eat caviar too don't you Miss High Class?"

"Well you would be right with that asinine assumption." If he was looking for a fight, I had a feeling he was about to get one.

"I suppose black folk don't eat caviar either?"

"No. No they don't. I guess you're just a special kind of black person." He let out a light laugh.

"Why does what I eat bother you so much?" I finally asked him.

"It doesn't bother me," he said piddling with his steak and losing eye contact with me.

"It obviously does. Everything I do, or eat for that matter surprises you, or you have something negative to say about it. Do you think that we as a people don't deserve to eat, have or do things that are deemed by others as the finer things in life?"

"It's not that. It's just that.. Well.."

"Well what? Out with it."

"You seem a little bourgeois is all."

"Bourgeois?" I laughed hysterically, not realizing how loud I had gotten. I leaned into Stuart and whispered into his ear, "So you think because I know I deserve the best that I'm bourgeois?"

I could tell that I had awakened something inside Stuart, because it was apparent enough that the hairs on the back of hands stood at attention and a knot formed in the middle of his throat. I looked at him. He was silent.

Cat got your tongue?" I asked. "Oh wait, don't tell me you don't eat pussy either?"

Stuart put his head in his hands. "I don't believe she just said that," he said to himself.

"Yes she did," I assured him. "Black people do say things like that. That I know for a fact." Stuart put a piece of steak in his mouth and looked at me in disbelief. I concluded that Stuart got his jollies by intimidating women. And I gathered they never gave him a run for his money. I made it very clear that I was not one of those women. I'm sure that my confidence turned Stuart on. He was still staring at me, still savoring the same piece of steak.

"So why *did* we lose touch on the Internet," he asked.

"You tell me, Playa, Playa." I rolled my neck.

"Oh now I'm a player," he chuckled.

"Well gigolo and pimp seemed to be played out. It's all that I can think of right now. You have to remember, I'm very observant, not much gets past me."

"You're a hard lady to get next to," he said.

"Get next to?" I asked offended.

"I see I really have to be careful what I say to you."

"That would be wise," I affirmed.

"I just mean.. Well I have been trying to talk to you for two years now, and it takes a job assignment for us to get together."

"Well you obviously haven't been trying hard enough."

"You're a control freak aren't you?"

"Typical."

"What is?" he asked.

"That because I am confident and know what I want in my life and refuse to settle, you would label me a control freak. Call me what you'd like. I really don't give a damn."

"Why the tough exterior?"

"That's your opinion," I told him. The waitress refilled my wine glass.

"Black folk don't drink wine with lunch either," he said, obviously trying to get a rise out of me.

"Coming from the oppressed black man," I sighed. We both laughed.

"I bet you don't believe that our people are oppressed either do you?" he asked.

"I believe that our people oppress their own selves."

"How do you figure that?"

"If *our* people," I said folding two fingers in gesture, "would just stop blaming everyone else for our problems, that would solve half of our issues."

"Give me a scenario," he said. He was really interested now.

"Well for instance. We complain that it is not our people that are bringing drugs into our communities. As much as this may be true, it doesn't mean we have to partake in it." Stuart had leaned back in his chair now, giving me his full attention.

"Let me ask you something Stuart."

"Shoot."

"If you were married, and you were away on a business trip let's say." I started using my hands. "And a woman took off her clothes and stood in front of you stark naked. Do you feel that the situation gives you the right to have sex with her? Or do you believe that it doesn't necessarily gives you the right, but blinds your better judgment?"

"No. I would make her leave or I would leave," he responded.

"*Exactly*, because *you* know that it's wrong, right. You have the power to decipher right and wrong for yourself," I said pointing my finger at him.

"Right."

"But one could argue that because he was tempted by the naked woman that he had no will power, therefore leaving him no choice but to fornicate with her." Stuart put his fork down, took a sip of water and wiped his mouth with his napkin. I continued.

"Then you would think that the people who are blaming other races for bringing drugs into the community would just simply not partake in those activities. Right?"

"Well it's not that easy."

"Sure it is."

"You don't understand, Renee. These are people who are at their lowest and have nowhere else to turn to."

"So they somehow think that using drugs; something they know is going to ruin their lives, is somehow better?" I raised my hands in disgust. "It doesn't make any sense. I just don't get it."

"I suppose you wouldn't. You had a silver spoon fed to you." Oh now those were fighting words.

"First of all, I wasn't born with a silver anything. I worked my butt off for everything I have." People in the restaurant started staring at us.

"Tell me something, Stuart. Were you born with a silver spoon in your mouth?"

"Not at all. I came out fighting."

"Exactly. So why is it that you aren't one of those people out there using the drugs."

"Because that is not the kind of life I wanted for....." I cut him off.

"Exactly. So you, like the rest of us, wanted the best out of life." The waitress placed our ticket on our table. I somehow sensed that she was hinting that it was time for us to leave their fine establishment. I didn't blame her. I was so engulfed in our conversation that I hadn't realized that I attracted more attention than I wanted to.

"It's four twenty. I think it would be okay for us to head out to DIA."

"How far is it from here?" he asked.

"About twenty-five miles," I answered. Stuart helped me out of my chair and escorted me outside. He opened my door and made sure I was in. He got in the car without saying a word. We drove about ten miles before I broke our silence.

"So tell me about San Diego," I finally said.

"San Diego is beautiful. Your kind of place."

"Oh?"

"Yes. Nice. Fancy. Expensive things. It's full of several independent nineties women such as yourself."

"You seem to have a problem with independent women such as myself." Oh brother here we go again.

"No, I have problem with women that think there is nothing on earth that men can do for them except fuck."

"Well actually, these days, women are fucking themselves or each other," I said as serious as a heart attack. "So we don't need men for that either." Stuart nearly ran off the road. I wanted to burst out laughing, but I kept my cool.

I continued, "I'm convinced men don't know what they want. They complain about a woman being too clingy or too needy, then when she gets a life of her own and puts herself in a position where she doesn't necessarily need a man, you guys have a problem." I got on a roll.

"Men get offended when they see women filling male roles, taking male jobs, or even get intimidated when they see a woman masturbating because now we've attacked their manhood, when they have left these very same women, to be single mothers, and fathers, for that matter, to their bastard children."

"That's not fair," Stuart disclaimed.

"Why isn't it fair? It's true isn't it?"

"It's not like that." I shook my head and thought to myself that this man has no clue.

"I guess being intellectually bankrupt would make one emotionally ignorant, don't you think?"

I must have really pissed him off because he pulled of the Pena Blvd exit and parked in the Holiday Inn parking lot. He got out of the car, slammed his door, and came around to my side and opened the door. I got out.

"No problem. I will take a cab to the airport and I can rent a car and still be on time to pick up Derrick."

"What are you talking about?" he shouted.

"Aren't you putting me out?"

"No. I am not. In spite of what you conceive of or believe about me. I'm a good guy. I wouldn't' put a lady out of my car."

"Then why are we stopping Stuart?" I said as if he was boring me.

"What is your problem Renee? You act like you don't need a man."

"I don't. And why does that bother you? Why does anything that pertains to me make a difference to you?" He ignored my question and lit into me.

"You stay up there on your high horse, and your holier than thou attitude as if you have the answers to everything." I didn't say a word. I just let him vent.

"Men actually want women to need them, to want them. We want to know that we will be allowed to rush to a woman's aid. We love women that embrace their femininity. We don't like hard women." I put my right hand on my chin and my left hand around my stomach.

"The bible says that the man is supposed to be the head. He is supposed to be the stronger sex, the provider." No he didn't go there with me.

"You tell that to the woman whose husband just left her for another woman and she now has to take care of four children on her own on welfare or she has to bust her ass and work two and three jobs to take care of them, which makes it hard for her to spend time with them. You tell that to the young woman who finds out that she is pregnant and the only thing the man that fathered the child has to say to her is that it's not his and that she is a whore. You tell that to the stupid man that has everything at home to lose, but thinks that a five-minute piece is worth far more than losing his family. You tell that to the sorry ass man who feels that beating his wife or girlfriend is a way to show her that he loves her. You tell that to a woman who is raped and abortion is not an option. And tell that to the wife who has contracted HIV from a husband who prefers dick over pussy. Don't you preach the bible to me buddy! I know it. If you're going to quote it, do it completely." I was hot and he knew it.

Stuart grabbed me by the waist. Now we were eye to eye. "Who hurt you?" he whispered. His whisper so close that his breath cause my bangs to flutter. It was actually somewhat breathtaking to me. I saw another side of Stuart. This wasn't his usual arrogant side. He ran his fingertips alongside my face. "What are you afraid of?" I knew that if this man didn't get out of my face, looking as fine as he did now, I was going to kiss him.

"Why are you so arrogant?" I said. That did it. He opened my door motioning me to get in. I got in and watched him walk around and get in the car. He slammed the car door shut and sped off into traffic. We drove the rest of the way to the airport in silence.

††††††

Derrick seemed disappointed when he realized that I wasn't alone.

"Renee," he said acknowledging my presence.

"Derrick," I acknowledged back. He looked in Stuart's direction. The look on his face told Derrick that he had missed the fireworks and that Stuart still steaming. Rejection is a motherfucker isn't it?

"Derrick, this is Stuart. Stuart, this is Derrick." I spotted a Starbucks Coffee. "Why don't you two get acquainted while I go and get a Café Mocha. Would either of you like anything?" They both declined.

When I got to Starbucks I ordered my Café Mocha with non-fat milk and four shots. As I waited for my cup of java, I observed Derrick and Stuart. They seemed to be entangled in an interesting conversation. Stuart's earlier stint had me curious. His physical persona fit my qualifications to a "T". However, I debated on whether or not he held any intellectual merit. Our prior conversation had left little to be desired. I hadn't been able to tell yet the level of his ambition. I guess I would just have to wait and see. I rejoined the two gentlemen; conversation already in progress.

"So uhhh, Stuart here tells me that you two met via the Internet," Derrick said.

"Something like that," I said. "We actually met at the gym, after we were put on this assignment together." I looked at Stuart.

"What's your favorite basketball team?" Stuart asked.

"Well it certainly isn't the Nuggets," I proudly proclaimed.

"Let me guess. You're a bandwagon Lakers fan right?" That was Derrick. He really should be seen and not heard.

"I've been a Los Angeles Lakers fan every since the early eighties. So if you call that a bandwagon fan, then a bandwagon fan I am. I've also been Dallas Cowboy fan since the seventies."

"Umph. A native Coloradoan, but you are a Los Angeles Lakers and a Dallas Cowboys fan. Go figure." That was big mouth Derrick again.

"What's your favorite baseball team?" Stuart asked.

"I don't do baseball."

"Hmm," was his response.

"But if it will make you feel any better, I do like the Colorado Avalanche."

"Hockey," they both said in unison, breaking out into loud laughter.

After we left the airport our plans were for Stuart and Derrick to drop me off at my hotel and they would go do the "guy" thing. I was happy to get rid of Derrick, but part of me wanted to be alone with Stuart. But then again, we'd probably only get into another negative debate. I wasn't in the mood for it.

I turned the shower in my hotel room on as hot as I could stand it. I really wanted to take a long hot bath, but would never do it in a hotel room. I stood straight under the showerhead as the water ran down my torso. I was anxious to get the Tech Expo over and head back to San Diego; my new home. I was missing Charlie, and wondered why he hadn't called me yet. I knew he was upset, but even though my intentions were not to hurt him, I knew that he was.

I wondered if I should visit my mother while I was in town. I knew I would be a bad daughter if I didn't check on her before I left. After I got out of the shower, I put on some jeans and a t-shirt and called my mother to let her know that I was in town for a few days. Drudgingly I picked up the receiver and dialed her number.

"Hello?" she answered.

"Hi mom, it's me."

"Who is me?" she asked knowing who it was.

"Renee," I replied.

"Oh you mean it' the daughter that left me and moved to San Diego?"

"Mom I didn't call to argue with you. I just wanted you to know that I am in town for a few days on business. Do you need anything while I'm here?"

She hung up. So much for that. I decided that since I had not heard from Charlie I would call him. I dialed his home number but the voice mail came on. I tried dialing his cell phone number. He picked up on the third ring.

"Hello, Luv," he said. "How are you?"

"Charlie I'm kind of concerned. I've been here since this morning and haven't heard a word from you. "

"I'm sorry, Luv, I've been taking care of some things here and getting things all squared away. Plus, Luv, to be truthfully honest, I've had a lot of things on my mind." I wondered if Charlie was going to express what he was feeling or leave me guessing.

"What things have you had on your mind?" I asked.

"Let's not worry about that right now. I just had to sort my feelings out. We'll talk about it when you get back.

"Where are you?"

"Your place. Is that okay?"

"Of course, I was just wondering. You weren't at home. That is why I called you on your cell phone."

"Yes I'm here all *alone* in this large house of yours." He made emphasis on alone.

"What have you been doing to keep busy?" I asked feeling a guilt trip coming on.

"Well, like I said I've been tying up some loose ends and enjoying your place." I wondered if Charlie staying at my place was his way of staying that much closer to me.

"You know, Luv," he interrupted my thoughts. "I had the most interesting conversation with a co-worker."

"Is that right?" I asked.

"Yes and this young fellow was very inquisitive about one Renee Mathews."

"Me?" I asked in surprised.

"Yes, you."

"Who would be inquiring about me and why?"

"Hmmm, let's just say one Mr. Stuart Humphries wanted to know a little *more* about you. It seems that he is quite taken by you."

"Oh brother," I said aloud, rolling my eyes to the back of my head.

"Seems like you two have known each other for quite some time."

"Correction," I said. "Stuart and I became acquainted over the Internet. I told you that. However, I didn't have physical contact with him until a few weeks ago at the gym. You know that," I said sarcastically. Charlie knew more than he was letting on. "And this was a few days after you told me we would be on assignment together."

"Ahhh I see. It looks like I'm not the only one smitten with you."

"I would hardly call it that."

"Well, with the questions he was asking, he is very interested."

"Questions like what?" I was curious now. Stuart had gone out of his way to ask Charlie about me.

"I think I'll leave that up to him."

"Charlie don't do that." He got silent for a moment.

"I miss you, Charlie," I tried to play him up.

"I miss you too, Luv."

"I really hate that I agreed to the Expo this year."

"I can imagine," his response dry. Charlie and I stayed on the phone for a few hours talking about nothing. That was another thing that I loved about Charlie. We could talk hours about nothing or something. Charlie always had something interesting to talk about, or something new to teach me. Each conversation, I learned something new and exciting.

"Well, Charlie, it's getting late. And since I have no car, I can't go out and get anything to eat. I really don't feel like room service. I think I'm going to have a bottle of V-8 and then I'm going to lay down and go to sleep."

"Okay, Luv, you get your beauty sleep, not that you need it. You have pleasant dreams and I will talk to you in the morning. What time are you supposed to be at the tech center?

"We're supposed to set up our booth by seven twenty."

"Ok, do you want a wake up call, Luv?"

"I would love nothing more than a wake up call from you Charlie."

"Goodnight, Luv. Pleasant dreams. Love.." He stopped short of the 'you'. He had hung up. I thought to myself once again the reasons that Charlie and I were not together. I felt so safe, comfortable and trusting with him. One day I would tell Charlie that I heard what his mother said from the kitchen that day. I would also tell him of the things in my past that stopped me from accepting his proposal. I took a drink of my V-8. Before I knew it. I was out like a light.

††††††

$\mathcal{T}$he next morning I was awakened by the telephone. I just knew it was Charlie. Much to my disappointment and pleasure, it was Stuart.

"Rise and shine, precious. Let's get this show on the road," he said with more glee than an elf in Santa's workshop.

"Where are you guys?" I asked him.

"In the atrium drinking coffee."

"I'll meet you two in about thirty minutes." Before I could hang up my cell, the hotel phone rang.

"Hello," I answered.

"Well gee Luv, I can't give you a wake-up call if you're on the phone."

"I know. I was on the phone with Stuart."

"Ahhh. So Stuart has priority calling?"

"I don't find that the least bit funny Charlie."

"Well it is to me. It appears that our little friend has a crush on you."

"God, I sure hope not," I said, "because I don't have a crush on him. Actually, I find him to be quite annoying."

"Aww just give him a chance. You might like him."

"Charlie Thatcher I can't believe you're trying to give me away."

"Hey I told you I just want you to be happy. If he makes you happy then I'm happy."

"Charlie I need to get up and get dressed and meet them downstairs." I was not interested in the direction this conversation was going. I had to actually shake the notion that Charlie was actually egging Stuart on to pursue me.

"I don't know why we didn't get two rentals cars. Oh well it's not like I have anywhere to go while I'm here. I called my mother, and she hung up on me."

"Do you want me to fly out?" There was he again trying to fix things for me.

"No Charlie, I don't need you to come to my aid every time I have a problem. I just want you to be there when I get there."

"I'll be here, don't worry. Good luck at the Expo. Call me when you get a chance, and if not I will talk to you soon."

After I hung up the phone, I took a ten-minute shower and then transformed into my gray business suit. I threw on some mascara and some lip-gloss, put my hair into a bun and was on my way out the door. When I got to the lobby Stuart and Derrick were sitting in the atrium drinking coffee.

"How do you like your coffee," Stuart asked.

"Sugar with lots of cream," Derrick emphasized.

"Why Derrick, how did you ever know?" Derrick just rolled his eyes. "Good morning to you too," I said to him.

"Thank you dear," I said to Stuart taking my coffee from his hand. We gulped down our coffee and headed to the Tech Center. We got to the tech center at seven o'clock and set up our booth. I admired once again the beautiful job that the printers had done on the flyers and the banner.

The turn-out at the three-day expo was a record for Charles Schwab. We accepted in seventy-eight billion in new dollars and twenty-seven million in existing dollars from existing accounts. We also broke our record for IRA, Sep-IRA and Keogh accounts.

"Next year should be even better," I said to the two gentlemen after I opened the last custodial account. "New tax laws are implementing new 529 plans next tax year. Either of you studied up on it yet?"

"Yea and I can see many of those custodial accounts converting," Stuart said.

"I've heard about them, but I've yet to really read up on them," Derrick said.

"Okay. I'm sure if you look on the Schwab University site, they should have a few classes that could help you better understand the product."

"I'll do that when I get back," Derrick had shocked me. I expected something more sarcastic from him. I was glad it was over and was anxious to get to the airport.

"How **was your** flight Luv," Charlie said when I claimed my luggage from the carousel.

"Considering I don't like to fly, it was alright."

Charlie chuckled, and for what seemed like ten minutes, Charlie stared at me, speechless. His gaze never left mine. I began to feel uncomfortable so I turned away and looked around the airport.

"So where'd ya park?" I asked. I turned back around to find that his gaze still hadn't left me.

"What's wrong?" I asked him.

"Nothing. I just love you so much is all." I hated when Charlie told me that. It only made things more difficult. "Let's get out of here," he said.

When we got to my house, Charlie opened the door and let me out of the car. I noticed that he had planted some flowers in the front yard.

"You know you didn't have to do that." I don't even know why I said it.

"Cover your eyes," he said ignoring me. My better judgment told me that Charlie had done something that he should not have. He guided me into the house and uncovered my eyes. I was in total awe. Charlie had completely decorated the whole place and much to my surprise, I loved it.

"You sure took a risk," I managed to say between my gawking.

"Id like to think that I know you pretty well. Besides, if you don't like it, you can always return it."

"Like hell I will. I love everything. Well except for the leopard vase."

Charlie laughed, "Somehow I didn't think you'd like it. But I liked it. You can't blame a guy for trying."

"Charlie, I appreciate this but why do you keep doing this?" My tone had become serious. I couldn't leave well enough alone.

As usual, he ignored me, "I didn't dare touch your bedrooms or the bathrooms. I know how you women are." I let it go. The last thing I wanted to do was say something to hurt him again.

"I really don't plan on sleeping on the floor tonight. Where can a lady get a bedroom suite around these parts?"

"I know just the place," he said. Before I knew it we were off. I admired the scenery as we drove from Coronado into San Diego.

"You mind letting your hair dance in the wind?"

"Let me make sure it's on tight," I joked.

"I have a bottle of glue in the glove compartment if you need it," Charlie said. We both laughed.

My cell phone rang. I looked at my display. It was Stuart. I put the phone back in my purse.

"Answer it," Charlie said.

"Nah, it's not important." Even though Charlie was acting like a good sport, I knew had I answered that phone it would have another dagger in Charlie's heart.

"So where are we going?"

"I think Helig Meyers is going out of business. You should be able to find something there. Do you know what you want?" he asked.

"I was thinking of something in a cherry oak perhaps. Four posters. Canopy. King Size."

Charlie looked at me. "King Size? Awful big bed for lil ole you." I realized that at that point Charlie was looking for a fight. I knew if we got into one, exceptional make up sex would follow.

"Yep. Did I ever tell you that since I was a little girl, I've wanted a king size bed, so I can jump up and down in it whenever I want and not have to worry about falling out of it?" Charlie looked at me as if I had just lost my last mental screw.

"Alrighty then."

††††††

*I***was trying** to get used to staying in this big house all by my lonesome. Since I had been in San Diego, Charlie had spent every night with me. Now that he was gone back to San Francisco, I had to learn to do things for myself. The one thing that I loved and hated about Charlie at the same time was that he spoiled me. I hadn't lifted a finger the entire time he was here. I went around the house dusting and placing things exactly where I wanted them. I heard my cell phone ringing from in the family room. I ran to answer it, hoping it was Charlie. I looked at the display. It was Stuart.

"Hello?" I answered.

"Well if I didn't know any better, I'd say that you were trying to avoid me Renee."

"You give yourself *way* too much credit?" I said.

"I've left you a whole bunch of messages and you haven't returned one of my calls."

"Honestly, Stuart, I wasn't aware that you called. I've had my phone off."

"I know better," he said sarcastically. "So is this a bad time, or do you just want me to stop calling you?"

"It's not that," I started. "I just..."

"Go out on a date with me," he interrupted.

"Well, I...don't know what to say," I was really trying to figure out a way to get out of this, but realized it wasn't happening.

"Just say yes."

"Yes," I blurted out.

"Have you been down to the Gaslamp Quarters yet?"

"Huh?" I said.

"I guess that answers my question. How does Friday at seven sound?"

"That's fine," I submitted.

"So are you busy right now?"

"No," I said.

"You feel up to chatting?"

"Sure. So what would you like to talk about?"

"Well I don't know. I guess we can get re-acquainted with each other."

"Damn," I shrieked.

"You okay over there?" he asked.

"Yes, I was watching the game."

"Which one?"

"Cowboys and the Eagles." Stuart burst out in laughter. I don't know what he saw so damn funny. I was a loyal fan but the Cowboys were working my last nerve. Dave Campo and Troy Aikman had to do something and had to do it quick because America's Team had turned into America's laughing stock.

"I'm glad you find that funny."

"I wasn't laughing *at* you, I was laughing *with* you,"

"Ha, Ha, Ha," I patronized.

"So now that we have concluded that you are a sports fan and you like the Dallas Cowboys and I know that you are a Los Angeles Lakers fan, what do you do in your spare time?"

"Work," I gave in short.

"Besides work. What gets your fire going?"
"Not arrogant men, they burn my nerves." Who am I kidding? I am actually attracted to Stuart, but I refuse to let him know that. I was serious about arrogant men being a turn off to me. But this one seemed to want to race with me, and I was ready on start, aiming to be the first one on the finish line. I told myself if I could get past his arrogance, that maybe I could search my soul to find out

just how much I liked him. I could tell he was destined to find out before I did.

"Seriously Renee. What are your passions in life? What are your long term life goals?"

"Hmm," was all I said.

"If you couldn't quit your job right now, what would be the one thing you would be content doing for the rest of your life?"

"Eating bon bons and watching 'All My Children' every day."

"You don't strike me as the bon bon or the soap opera type. But hey, looks can be deceiving."

"You should know," I mumbled. "Writing," I said before he could respond to the last nasty comment I had made.

"Excuse me?" Stuart asked.

"Writing. My passion is writing."

"What kind of writing?"

"What ever trail my imagination leaves at the tip of the pencil as it glides on the paper."

"Hmmm. Do you have anything published?" I was somewhat embarrassed that I entered a short story last year and won first prize. I had gone on Fastweb.com and signed up for various scholarships and writing contests. I saw the one for Playboy and thought what the heck. The first prize was fifteen hundred dollars and publication. My imagination ran away with me and that very imagination won me a much needed fifteen hundred dollars.

"Yes," I said.

"That's great. What was it?"

"A short story in Playboy."

"Are you serious?"

"Yep," was all I said, waiting for him to judge me.

"That's cool. Maybe one day you'll feel comfortable enough to share it with me."

"Maybe, maybe not."

"Renee?"

"Stuart?"

"Why are you so cold towards me? You don't have to play hardball with me," Stuart said.

"I don't know what you are talking about. I think we're getting along quite well considering." Although I knew very well what he meant. I had figured out a long time ago that I had built up this wall when it came to men, especially black men. It wasn't like I had any positive male role models in my life. I had no idea who my real father was. Men I had dealt with left much to be desired. I was tired of giving and not getting. Living in Denver, I found that brothers were intimidated by me, therefore they used whatever opportunity available to try and tear me down.

"Your degree and money don't make you no betta than me honey," one had told me after I told him I would rather he not have my phone number.

"Why don't you just take it as me not being attracted or interested in you, instead of you making it out to be something it is not," I had said back.

"I'm not hard, I'm just cautious," I said diverting my attention back to Stuart. "Just cautious."

"I'm going to be honest with you. I am very interested in you and I'm very attracted to you. Always have been. I want to become friends and see what comes out of it."

"I thought we were friends, Stuart."

"Renee, you know what I mean. I have been trying to get to know you since we first met on the Internet."

"Ha!" I said.

"What's that supposed to mean?" he asked, acting innocent.

"You know damn well what I mean MrTrueGent. Your name should have been MrTruePlaya," I laughed. I used to sit in the chat room that we frequented and watch him make his rounds trying to get with as many women as he could. He was smooth and good, but only for someone that was weak and desperate. So needless to say, when he got to me, ChkltCity, he was at a dead end. I wasn't falling for his game.

"I can't believe that you thought I was a player."

"Think you are a player. As in present tense."

"Come on now, give me the benefit of the doubt. That was a chat room."

"Umhmm," was all I said.

"I still remember a lot of things about you," he said trying to make brownie points.

"Humor me." I asked.

"I know that your favorite color is purple." Right. "I know that your favorite perfume is White Diamonds." That used to be my favorite perfume. "I know you are a computer geek." Right again. "I know that you don't get along with your mother." Okay he had crossed the line.

"My favorite color *is* purple. My favorite perfume is Organza by Givenchy. And as far as my mother, that's none of your gotdamn business." It was too late. I had said it. I didn't mean to snap at Stuart like I had. The mention of my mother just pissed me off.

"Look Renee, I don't want to upset you and it looks like this phone conversation is not going the way I had planned. How about I give you a break until Friday and then we see how it goes then?"

"Sounds good," I said.

"Okay, get some rest, and have a good week."

"Stuart?"

"Yes?"

"I'm sorry for snapping at you. If we become close, maybe one day I'll let you see past the layers."

"Deal," Stuart said. "Goodnight Renee."

"Goodnight."

After I hung up the phone I stretched out on my sofa and wondered myself exactly what it was that I was so scared of. I mean I'm a good woman. I have a lot going for me. I was in high demand. But experience had taught me that everything that looks good to you is not good for you.

My mother never had a stable relationship. As a matter of fact the only relationship that I had seen my mother in was an abusive one. She stayed with Leon for fifteen years and endured daily beatings for little or no reason. I never dared asked my mother why she stayed and put up with that nonsense, but I heard her on several occasions on the telephone telling her friends that he the reason was because he helped her take care of Eddie and me and paid the bills. I refuse to stay with an abusive man because he's taking care of me financially. My mother had always told me that I was ignorant when it came to men.

"You got all this criteria for a man, that's why you ain't neva' gone have no man."

"Mama why should I settle and belittle myself just for the sake of being with a man?"

"Let me tell you something Renee just as long as you understand the three F's of keeping a man, you'll be able to keep a man."

"What are the three F's," I asked her curiously. By hook or by crook I knew that sex had something to do with it.

"Feed 'em, fuck 'em and," she paused for a moment. "I forgot the third one, but you get my point."

I rolled my eyes at my mother. "It's forget them."

"Feed 'em, fuck 'em and forget 'em?" That don't make no damn sense Renee." I really felt sorry for her. I wanted more than that from a relationship. If all I had to offer a man was to feed him and fuck him, I didn't have much to offer a man. I wanted a relationship that was headed by God.

"What about love mama?" I had asked her.

"Love? Girl, you sillier than I thought you was. Love don't love nobody. And no matter how much a man says he loves you, you best believe he tellin' his Saturday and Sunday woman the same thang. If you don't learn nothin' else I done taught you, you remember this one thang. All black men are the same. I don't care what they tell you, they black ass is lyin'. It may not happen right away but he gone eventually fuck up. That's what they do Nae, fuck up for no fuckin' reason at all. So, since you can't do nothin' bout it, you just get what you need out of it."

"Mama, you would stay with a man knowing he is also with other women? I don't get that. Why would someone do something so foolish?"

"Nae, you got a lot of growing up to do. I just hope you do it real soon or you gone have a hard way to go." I shook my head and looked at my mother all the while telling God that I didn't want to be like her. I asked him to give her the revelation that she could do bad all by herself.

I came to the conclusion that my mother was emotionally content. In the beginning of her relationship with Leon, my mother went through the ordeal of dealing with his murder trail. He was accused of killing a white woman. The prosecutors said that he stabbed the woman several times in the front seat of his 1973 Monte Carlo. Even though they found blood on the seats, he got off on circumstantial evidence.

Even after the mayhem had subsided my mother stayed with Leon. She stayed with him fourteen years after that and Leon eventually stopped coming around. And to my mother's best interest. Three years ago Leon was sentenced to the death penalty for being caught in the act of stabbing a woman thirty two times in the front seat of his car.

During the trial, inserts from his journal were read and in one of his entries, he stated that each time he stabbed that poor woman; he thought he thought about my mother. God was sure looking down on her.

No, I would not be like my mother. I'd make better choices in my life, especially when it came to men. And most importantly, if I ever got married, my relationship with my children would be much different and better by far. Unlike my mother, I would love my children and encourage them, instead of tear them down and diminish their self worth, and I would always be there for them.

I went upstairs to my room and prepared myself a luxurious bubble bath. Complete with milk and shea butter. I had told Charlie I wanted one of those Bose stereo system installed in the walls throughout the house, and like always Charlie had come through.

I selected a CD that I had burned specifically for those moments when I wanted to be alone. It had Norman Brown, Gerald Levert, Will Downing, Kenny Lattimore as well as a few other crooners to my liking. I took a bottle of wine from the wet bar that lay discretely underneath the cabinets. I pulled my hair up into a banana clip and slid into the sudsy paradise.

The water was hotter than I had liked but it felt good against my aching muscles. I hadn't kept on my workout regimen since I had been in San Diego, but had planned on joining 24 Hour Fitness as soon as time permitted. I had been in San Diego, all but three weeks, and already, it felt like home. I knew this is where I would stay. I knew this is where I would call home.
A few days earlier, Charlie had taken me car shopping. I had thought about getting a Lexus, but settled on a E500 Sedan. My color of choice was gold.

I slid further into the hot, sudsy water until my mouth was nearly emerged in the water. This felt so good. *Mmmmm.*

Chapter 9

It's Friday morning and I need to buy something to wear on this date with Stuart. Part of me really didn't want to go, but I knew I needed to go, even if it was just to get out of the house. I found my way in my new Mercedes down to Mission Valley Mall. I had never been to a mall, where the entrance to all the stores were on the outside instead of being housed in a large enclosed structure.

I stopped at Robinson's May first. I didn't see anything I liked except a hat and a pair of earrings. Next I was off to Victoria's Secret; although the thought of being intimate with Stuart never crossed my mind. LOL. Okay, I'm lying, but not on our first date. However, you just don't buy a new outfit and not buy the matching intimate apparel.

I was running low on my supply of Organza so I decided to pick it up at Macy's. Once at Macy's I saw this "to die for" little black number. I decided to stop by Nine West to get my shoes on the way out of the mall. .

Okay, now I'm standing in the parking lot and have everything I need to look the bomb tonight, but I feel like I'm forgetting something. I look down at my toes. Of course I had to get a French pedicure. I looked at my watch. It was four thirty and my date with Stuart was at seven.

After I got my toes done I rushed home to get ready. I had just a little under an hour before Stuart arrived. I showered, shaved, oiled myself down and got dressed. I put on some face powder, eyeliner, mascara and a mauve lip-gloss to finish my face. My doorbell rang. I looked at the clock in my bedroom; it was six fifty seven. Stuart was prompt. He had been awarded his first brownie point.

Had he been five minutes late, he would have been going on the date by himself.

"Wow," was all he said when I opened the front door. He didn't look too shabby himself. He had on a pair of tan linen pants and a darker brown silk shirt that button up the front, with a pair of brown leather Stacey Adams. I wondered to myself why I had chosen black. Oh well, it was too late now.

"Well, are you going to sit there and stare at me all night?" I said, breaking the silence. "By the way, the drool is so becoming." We both laughed.

"Renee. You look absolutely stunning."

"You don't look too bad yourself," I teased. "Yea, wash you down with a hose and throw a few threads on you, and complete it with some Old Spice, you look halfway decent."

"Old Spice?" he looked surprised. I rolled my eyes at him. "Are you ready silly?" he asked.

"Yes Sir." With that we were off in Stuarts black Mercedes SLK convertible. As usual the Coronado scenery was beautiful, and the San Diego skyline was even more beautiful as we approached downtown.

"Reservation for two for Humphries," Stuart told the waiter once we arrived at a restaurant called Aqua Al 2.

"Aqua Al 2?" I said aloud.

"It's pronounced, ah-qwa-all-do-eh," he explained.

"Aquaallduah," I tried.

Stuart chuckled and said, "No, repeat after me. "Ah."

"Ah."

"Qwa."

"Qwa."

"All."

"All."

"Do."

"Do."

"Eh."

"Eh."

"By George I think she's got it,' Stuart teased me. I squeezed his forearm. Good Lord what did I do that for? Stuart had some of the most muscular arms. A flicker of heat came over me. I cleared my throat as Stuart and I followed the waiter to an outside table. I had never been to a restaurant where I dined outside. Living in Colorado, left one culturally enslaved and socially bound.

"Nice choice," I complimented Stuart.
"I'm glad it's to your liking Renee. Ms. Matthews if you're nasty."
"I'm not so it's Renee to you." I could tell that Stuart had a habit of putting his foot in his mouth and didn't have any idea on how to stop the trend.

"You know I'm joking," he said.

"Are you?" I said looking him straight in his eye. I must have made him nervous because he nearly choked on his Cabernet. For a few moments he found it hard to look me in my face.

I asked Stuart a few questions about the Gaslamp District and he schooled me on its importance to San Diego history. I also learned that Stuart was originally from the bay area and had moved to San Diego in 1987 after an honorable discharge from the Marines. The fact that Stuart was seventeen years older than me made him more attractive to me. I definitely had the "older man" syndrome.

We continued with our conversation and I couldn't help but pay attention to the scent he had on. It was very pleasant, and somewhat sexy. The entire tête-à-tête, I kept complete eye contact with Stuart, which often left a crack in his voice.

"You like intimidating men don't you?"

"Me? Intimidate men? Come on now. Where would you get such a silly idea?" I asked trying to sound guiltless. I knew what he meant though. It wasn't that I tried to intimidate men; I just looked at men for what they were. I could see right through most, no matter what they said. It was my way of letting them know that it is was not what they said, but what they did; all the rest was bullshit to me. And it irked me when I was talking to someone and they looked everywhere but in my face.

"The way you look at me for example, when we are talking. It's almost as if you're staring right through me, sizing me up."

"I am. Is that a bad thing? Are you afraid that I might see something that you don't want me to?" His silence told me that I wasn't far from the truth. I broke it by saying, "I'm just an attentive person. You were talking, I was listening."

"You're a hard one to read Renee," he gave up.

"And that, my dear, is a good thing," I assured him. "So where do you live?" I asked.

"In Mission Valley," he responded.

"I think I know where that is. I was at the mall today. That's off of I-8 right?"

"You've got it," Stuart said eying me up and down. "So uh... you bought this little number just for your date with me?" he asked. His arrogance had reared its ugly head again. Will this fool ever learn?

"Don't flatter yourself, I am a shoe addict and Victoria Secret had thongs on sale," I bet that will shut him up. He gulped. Umhmm serves his black ass right. Now he has to wonder all night if I was wearing a pair of thongs or not, knowing that he wasn't getting any.

After watching me eat and smiling at me for a couple of moments, he asked me, "Have you been to the beach on Coronado after a beautiful sunset?"

"Yes I have." His eyebrows were now raised.

"Oh really? Not usually a place where someone goes alone."

"I would agree," I said, leaving him wondering.

"So are you seeing someone?" he tried another approach.

"No," I said blandly. I knew it was eating him up inside wondering who it was that I went to the beach with.

"So I guess taking you there again would be out of the question?"

"No, I love it, and it's close to home."

After the waiter had returned with Stuart's credit card, he helped me from my seat and we exited the restaurant. On the way out the same waiter handed Stuart a carryout bag.

"Still hungry eh?" I teased.

"Something like that," he whispered behind the nape of my neck. My legs immediately turned into two limp noodles. Good lawd, he had a way of bringing my hormones to life. But there was no way in hell I was about to let him know that.

Moments later we pulled into a parking lot and got out of the car. We walked to a secluded part of the beach. The breeze from the water, although cool, was welcomed.

"You may want to take off those expensive shoes, unless you're afraid to get those pretty little toes dirty." I don't know what he was talking about; the sand had already invaded my shoes and my toes. What the heck, I squatted down to unbutton my straps.

"No, no, let me," Stuart insisted. He kneeled down in front of me and ran his finger in a circular motion around my ankle as he unbuttoned my straps. I was sure that had I not worn any panties, my legs would have been home to a stream of hot liquid.

I admired the water the same way I had done the first time I had come here with Charlie. The shade of indigo was just breath taking. The sound was serene, yet alive. The crumbling of paper broke my concentration as I fixed my eyes on Stuart. He had brought the bag that he had gotten from the restaurant. I just know he's not about to break out and eat right here in front of me. My mood was killed, until a spoon met my mouth with the tastiest cheesecake I had ever had.

"Umm," I said. "How'd you know I love cheesecake."

"I know."

"How do you know?"

"Let's just say that you're not the only one that has listening and attention skills." There was cockiness again. Boy does he ever learn?

After more conversation, I learned that Stuart's favorite colors were silver and gold, not to be construed with the "bling bling", although he did wear a diamond stud in his left ear. I also learned that he loved Jazz and he loved him some Etta James.
Stuart had a daughter in college from a previous relationship. I could tell that he was very proud of his daughter; she was taking pre-med at Stanford. His parents had moved back to West Virginia where he had visited at least twice a year. I envied him in a way, having a two-parent home and being able to visit his parents who were still together in such happiness.

Stuart told me that he had turned his life over to Christ a few years ago. Now he had my attention.

"Tell me about that." I wanted to hear his story.

"Hmmm. Well I was brought up in the church, Baptist, but I had no idea of the real reason I should be seeking Christ. One New Year's Eve I was sittin' in a club women watching." I rolled my eyes. "There were lots of hotties up in there that night. Hotties such as yourself of course," he smirked. I raised my eyebrow at him in disapproval.

"I'm not laughing," I assured him.

"I'm joking. So, anyway, I thought to myself that this was getting boring. I wanted more in my life. I made money, but that's all I had going for me. I just felt empty and wanted God to make an impact on my life." Now we were getting to the core; something that really mattered. He continued.

"I left that club and headed straight to one of the local churches. I made it just before midnight and brought the New Year in as a new man who had re-dedicated his life to Christ."

"Are you active in church now?"

"Yes. I am actually in the choir and in the men's and single's ministry." He was really holding my attention. The more he talked about his relationship with God, the more I wanted to know.

"So what church do you go to?"

"North Park Apostolic Church."

"Apostolic? I've never heard of that."

"It's a little different, we are word and works based. Our teachings are based on the books of Acts. Maybe one day you can stop in and see if you like it."

"I just might do that. I haven't even given a church home a second thought since I've been here."

"Did you attend church back home?"

"Yes I attended Now Faith Christian Fellowship Church in Denver. Have you ever heard of Joe Pace and the Colorado Mass Choir?"

"Stir up the gift. Lay ya hands on *meee* Lord!" Stuart began to sing. I was impressed at his voice.

"You can sing," I complimented him. I told him about all the women having a crush on Joe Pace.

"There was this one snobby girl, her name was Valerie and she was best friends with the preacher's daughter."

"A beneficial position to be in," Stuart said.

"You're right, because neither of them could do any wrong. But Valerie was so positive that she and Joe were going to get married, even down to the two-carat engagement ring he had bought her. I'm sure eventually he saw what everyone else saw. But much to my surprise, one day I was reading JET Magazine and Joe had married himself a doctor in Alabama."

"And I'm sure old Valerie was crushed." Stuart finished. I chuckled.

"Umhmm."

"Who's your favorite gospel artist?" Stuart asked me.

"I'd have to say Fred Hammond by far," I said excited.

"Yes, Fred is good."

"And yours?"

"I'd say Fred is up there. Kirk for sure. And let me see. CeCe does a hit and miss, but I love me some Debbie and Angie. Those are my girls."

"Yea I like them too. *Bold* was off the hook." We sat a little while longer discussing our likes and dislikes and I came to the conclusion that without his arrogance and cockiness, Stuart was a pretty cool guy. I got home about 3:00 a.m.

"I actually had a nice time," I told Stuart once he walked me to my door.

"You doubted that you would?"

"Yes. Truthfully I only went out with you to shut you up. But I'm glad I did." Stuart chuckled, took my hand and placed the softest kiss on it.

"Goodnight Renee." Oh Lord, he did it again. Somebody help me.

"Goodnight Stuart."

I shut the door and fell to the floor. My feet were dirty from the sand and I could feel the stickiness underneath my dress. I hadn't expected to have a good time with Stuart. I was actually impressed. Although I liked his style, I still wasn't completely bent on him. He was smooth and he was good at it. If he had foul intentions I would certainly be playing his game with him and in the end he would be the one that came out played.

I turned on the faucet in the shower got undressed and checked for messages. It concerned me that Charlie had not called me since he left except to say that he had

made it home safely. He knew I would worry if he hadn't.
I wanted to call him but decided to give him some space.
I hoped I would never lose Charlie as a friend. I showered
and fell asleep.

Chapter 10

The doorbell was ringing. I looked over at my clock; it was 9:17 a.m. I put on my robe and walked downstairs to answer the door. It was the florist accompanied by a beautiful bouquet of red roses. I was sure they were from Charlie, but they weren't. They were from Stuart. *They're not lilacs, but like you, they are equally beautiful*, was written on the card.

I tipped the florist, closed the door and carried the roses to the kitchen and placed them in a vase. My cell phone was beeping. I checked the messages. There were three, one from the human resources at the office, one from Office Depot, they were confirming my appointment today to set up my home office.

The third message was from Stuart. He said he had a good time last night and hopes to have many more good times with me. We'll see.

I had painted my home office the week before. It was various shades of purple. On one of the walls I had painted a lilac mural. I did a pretty good job if I must say so myself. Charlie tried to talk me out of it until he saw the finished product. I had ordered all cherry oak furniture; a desk with a hutch and shelving for all of the hundreds of books had collected over the years. They ranged from novels, computer manuals, psychology, and politics to religion, self help and english.

I had two computers and a laptop, four printers and a slew of other pieces of office equipment. Although I felt like home in San Diego, I felt uneasy about the installers from Office Depot coming by while I was there alone. I took a chance and called Stuart on his cell phone.

"Stu speaking," he answered.

"Stu?" I mimicked. I chuckled.

"Oh I'm sorry, I was trying to reach the politically correct black man that read me the riot act in Benihana's."

"Hey sweetie," he said laughing. He knew he would never hear the end of this.

"Hey you," I said. "Thank you for the roses, they were beautiful. But you didn't have to."

"There you go. It hurts you to have a man do something for you doesn't it?"

"No, I'm just saying you didn't have to." Stuart knew he didn't want to go a round with me this morning so he changed the subject.

"So to what do owe this call to?" he asked.

"Well I needed a favor."

"Oh My Lord, she needs something, she wants something from a man! There is a God." My first inclination was to hang up on his ass. I decided against it.

"Office Depot is coming by soon to set up my home office, and I don't really want to be here alone, when they get here."

"What time are they coming?"

"Between now and three."

"Okay, I can be there in about forty five minutes. Is that okay?"

"Yes that is fine."

"If they get there before I do, and you start to get uncomfortable, just throw out there that your husband should be home soon."

"You wish," I said. He just never lets up.

"No, I pray," he said hanging up the phone. What an ass I thought.

Stuart arrived before the installers did. I had cut up some fresh fruit and put it on a tray with little finger sandwiches.

"Are you hungry?" I asked.

"No I caught a bite to eat earlier." I gave him the once over. He was dressed in a tan suit. Impressive if I must say so myself.

"Is there anywhere I can hang my jacket," he said taking off his sports coat.

"Umm no, leave that on, you wont' be staying that long. I don't want you to get too comfortable." I was laughing on the inside, and the look on his face was priceless.

"I'm kidding Stuart," I said after I realized he didn't think what I had said was funny at all. I hung his jacket in the foyer closet.

"This is really nice," he said. "I know you can't afford this even on Schwab's salary. You an undercover drug dealer?"

"No, and now you're in my business."

"I was joking," he said.

"I wasn't," I said back. He rolled up his sleeves on his shirt and walked around admiring the house.

"I see you like black art as well. I have a lot of Ashton's work, but I'm looking to make a change. I'm kind of tired of it."
This man was fine, saved and had some style and class. Another brownie point.

"I'm afraid to ask what it looks like upstairs. You might think I might want to try and get you into bed."

"Honey, you couldn't get me into bed, even if you wanted to." I rolled my eyes at him and walked up the staircase. I turned around and he was still standing at the bottom. "Are you coming?"

"I wasn't given permission."

I turned completely around and looked down at him. "Follow me my little pet." He followed. While I was showing him around, the doorbell rang.

"Get the door. *Husband.*" I didn't look at him, but I could imagine the look on his face. I heard him laughing to himself on the way down the stairs. After the installers had completed my office I was pleased. Stuart and I decorated and put things in their perspective places. We were both exhausted.

"You read all these books?"

"Most of them," I answered.

"In Search of Mrs. Goodpussy?" he raised his eyebrow at me.

"Just like a man. That's the first book you see. It's not even about what you think." He still wasn't convinced. I found myself having to explain myself.

"Its overtone is not about sex," I said. "It's about manhood. What men want from women and themselves and life in general."

"You mean to tell me that there is not one mention in here about pussy?" he asked. I let out a burst of laughter.

"Well there is one chapter in there. I believe it's the chapter that shatters the myth that black men don't eat sushi."

"You're too much for me," he said putting his face in his hands.

"I've been telling you that for the longest."

"I better get back home. I'm about to fall out," he said.

"You can crash on the couch if you'd like until you get enough energy to go home." What in the hell did I say that for? I couldn't believe I said it. But I did.

"As tempting as that is, I'm going to have to take a rain check. However, if you're not busy later on tonight, I wouldn't mind seeing you again. I mean if that's okay with you."

"What did you have in mind?" I asked him.

"Well, I can cook; really well. And I want to cook dinner for you."

"You can't cook. This is California. Most folks here can't cook, that's why they eat out so much."

"Your sense of humor never ceases to amaze me. But I really *can* cook. My mother taught me." Ahh sookie. He can cook and his mother taught him. I was going to have him put his money where his mouth was."

"Okay you've got a deal." Stuart gave me directions to his house and was out the door.

†††††††

*I***knew going** to Stuart's house was trudging on some serious territory, so I made sure I looked as un-appealing as possible. I threw on some jeans and a Dallas Cowboy jersey, complimented by my Fila tennis shoes. I threw my hair back into a ponytail and put on a baseball cap. This should do the trick. After this, I won't have to worry about him trying to *mack* me anymore.

I was impressed with the neighborhood that Stuart had me venture into. Some of the houses were bigger than mine, some the same size as mine and some smaller than mine. I ventured up the hill on Del Rio Camino Lane and ended up in front of a row of private town homes. I searched for 2782 and pulled up front of its garage. I rang the doorbell. Stuart answered the door wearing an apron that said, *Californians cook it best.* I laughed.

"Ohh that's hideous," I chuckled.

"And hello to you too." He let me in and I must say I was all the more impressed with Stuart. His furniture was all black accented with silver wrought iron. Sure enough about three or four Ashton's graced his walls. Everything was so clean and neat, nearly spotless.

"You can sit here, or you can come into the kitchen with me. I'm almost done. Whichever makes you feel comfortable."

"I think I'll watch you in the kitchen to make sure you haven't ordered some take out and trying to pass it off as your own." He chuckled, his dimples as apparent as a fat person in spandex. I don't know how I missed his dimples before. His smile was strong and sexy, yet warm and protective.

I followed him into the kitchen. Dear Jesus, why are you torturing me like this? Stuart had on a pair of jeans and a black muscle shirt that clung to his every ripple. Jesus, Jesus, Jesus. I need to get on my knees right now and repent, cause the thoughts that I am having right now are not right. He had cut all his hair off and was bald.

"When did you cut your hair?"

"Wow, for someone to be so attentive and observant, you aren't doing very well. I cut my hair a few days ago. Which means it was cut when I came over earlier today."

I non-challantly threw my hand in the air, "Oh. Didn't notice." I know I was wrong for that, but I had to do something that would distract me. A little miniature mini-me sat on my right shoulder saying, "lick him, lick him". Jesus I wanted to do that and a number of other things. Lord *please* give me a reason to leave. God must have either been out on a potty break or laughing his tail off because I ended up staying.

Stuart was cooking seafood in an Alfredo sauce with pasta and fresh steamed vegetables. The aroma smelled so inviting. I watched Stuart as he put a little pinch here, dabbled a little there and tasted in between. He really knew his way around a kitchen.

I kept watching him; and his body. Beads of sweat started to form on his dark baldhead. The veins popped from his arms as he stirred the pot. His chest looked like that of a body building God. I couldn't believe that a man nearing fifty took such good care of himself.

He walked to the cabinet and paused for a moment. The way he was wearing those jeans; umph umph umph. The way the denim fitted his buttocks and wrapped around his thighs. The curve in his back made me want to run my tongue from the top to the bottom. I begin fanning myself as he turned around.

"You okay," he asked.

"Yes, just a little hot is all."

"That's funny, I was just looking for the cayenne pepper. I know I have some somewhere." If he only knew.

"I'll leave the pepper out if you'd like."

"Oh no, I love spicy food." And spicy men. I had to excuse myself because I was seconds away from pushing him to the floor and having my way with him.

"Can I use your restroom please?" I asked.

"Sure. I trust that you can find it." I left the kitchen, in good timing too. I went into the bathroom, shut the door behind me and leaned on the door. I sighed and wondered why was I here. I knew I was playing with fire and if I didn't play my cards right, I could get burned.

I splashed some cold water on my face and took a few deep breaths. His bathroom looked cleaner than mine. The leopard motif was very impressive. I gathered myself, touched up my powder and lip gloss, and went back out to the kitchen.

"You find it okay," he asked.

"Yes, thanks," I said. "You have a nice place here. Very impressive for a man."

"Not all men are slobs ya know?" Most of them are, I thought to myself. "Would you like a glass of wine?"

"Whatcha got?" I asked, just knowing all he had to offer was some cheap Zinfandel.

"Have you ever tried Moscoto?" I was impressed.

"Moscoto's my favorite wine." The eeriness of Stuart and I having too much in common was making me uncomfortable.

Stuart poured two glasses of wine and we both retreated to the butter crème leather sofa in the living room. He looked at me and burst out in laughter.

"What? Do I have a booger in my nose or something?"

His laughter was harder now.

"No, not that. I just can't get over you being a Dallas Cowboy fan."

"Don't hate, participate," I joked. I was in the middle of laughter when I felt his tongue invade my mouth. I should have pulled away. I didn't. I obliged his invitation to kiss me. When he pulled back, I could hardly breath.

"Renee," he said in the softest voice I had heard from a man. I was still trying to catch my breath. "Look, I'm not going to lie to you. I am falling for you."

Screeeeech! Stop rewind. Now why did he have to go and say something like that? I tried to find some sort of distraction; and quickly. My eyes landed on his CD collection. I walked over to it and admired it.

"Aren't we just a wee bit eclectic?" I asked. He had everything from David Sanborn to The Clark Sisters; Steely Dan to The Brothers Johnson.

"Nice," I said. Before I knew it I could feel Stuarts heated breath on the back of my neck. I froze. Why did he have to go and complicate things?

"Why do you keep running from me?" he whispered. I nearly fainted. "Am I such a bad guy, that you won't give me a chance?" For once in my life I was completely, utterly speechless.

"Renee?"

"What?"

"Turn around and look at me." I hesitated but turned around and met his gaze. The last time I felt this vulnerable was when I was a teenager and my mother had beat me to oblivion when she found out that I had gotten my grant money and hadn't given it to her.

"Tell me you're not attracted to me," he said. His breath blew my bangs across my face.

"I'm not attracted to you," I lied, holding my head down. He knew I was lying.

"You don't lie very well Nae," he called me Nae. I knew this was serious. "You want me just as much as I want you," he continued. "I've fallen in love with you and that scares you."

"You don't scare me," I hissed.

"No, but the fact that you could possibly feel the same for me, does scare you."

"So they teach psychology in the military?"

"Stop fighting it. Give it a chance. My intentions towards you are only good. Let me love you." My gaze was stuck on his, and as much as my mind told me to slap him and leave his place, my heart froze me.

"You can't love me the way I want to be or deserve to be loved."

"How do you know? You haven't given me a chance."

"Because no man can. No man can love me the way God loves me. No man can love me the way I love myself."

"Just give me a chance," he whispered brushing his hand across my cheek. "Just give me a chance." He bent down to kiss me. I don't know where the hell my mind was, but it was long gone, because my heart actually gave me the nerve to kiss him back. We kissed for what seemed like hours. He gently held my face in his hands as he explored the insides and outsides of my mouth.

I had never felt this way before. Even when I kissed Charlie with passion, although it sent chills down my spine, it didn't curl my toes and make all my other body parts go crazy.

"Why are you doing this?" I asked breaking our connection.

"Because I'm in love with you Ms. Matthews."

"You don't even know me."

"I know a lot more about you than you think I do." He took my hand and led me to the kitchen. "Let me spoil you," he said sitting me down in a wrought iron chair. I didn't say a word because I knew my mouth would get me in more trouble than I cared to be in. I just looked at him, never taking my eyes from him.

"You can try to look through me all you want. Whether you like it or not, this is something that even *you* can't control." He fed me. I kept my eyes on him, until I realized that I was tipsy from the wine. Or maybe I was tipsy on the natural high he had put me on. Either way, I was high.

"You're not driving home tonight," he said, moving the glass of wine from my reach.

"I'm not staying here," I said with much attitude.

"Yes you are," he said in a demanding demeanor.

"Like hell I am. You've lost your damn mind too,"

"If I wanted to try something with you, I would have already done it. You're going to sleep in my bed and I'm going to sleep out here on the couch."

I laughed with great cockiness. "I was wondering when the real you was going to show up," I was pissed off. Before I knew it, he had picked me up and swept me across his shoulder carrying me into his bedroom. I ranted and raved the entire time.

"Nae, calm down. I don't want you driving home in this condition."

"In what condition?"

"You've had too much to drink."

"I'm fine," I protested.

"You can sleep in your clothes, or you can sleep in this." He handed me one of his dress shirts. He kissed me on the forehead. "Goodnight," he said and disappeared on the other side of the closed door.

I sat on the edge of his bed looking around his immaculate bedroom. Like the main bathroom, it had a leopard motif. I especially admired the large statue of a spotted cheetah that sat on a long table at the foot of his bed. I stood by the door to see if could hear any movement in the other room. The television was on CNN and I could hear clacking in the kitchen. Stuart was cleaning dishes from our dinner. The wine I had drunk kicked up another notch, taking my buzz to another level of high. I knew that I had no business driving in this condition, so I put on the shirt that he offered me. Before I knew it, I was in dreamland.

††††††

*I***was awakened** the next morning to the smell of pancakes, bacon and eggs. I opened the bedroom door and walked into the kitchen.

"Good morning sleepy head. How did you sleep?" Stuart asked, smiling at me.

I stood at the entrance to the kitchen for a moment then walked to the cabinet and picked a strawberry from the plate of fruit he had prepared.

"You know, you look good in my shirt." I shot him a callous look.

He saw my concern and said, "Don't worry, there is a time and a place for everything. Like our wedding night." I rolled my eyes and eyed the spread that he had made.

"Don't be rollin' yo eyes at me missy. You're going to be Mrs. Stuart Humphries. I already asked God and He already said so."

"Well I didn't receive that memo because God ain't told me nothin'."

"First time I heard *ain't* come out your mouth. Perhaps there is some black in you after all." I walked out the kitchen; I knew he was watching me.

"When you get ready to take a shower, towels and everything are in the master bathroom," he called from behind me.

I turned in his direction and said, "My bad, I thought you only had one bathroom."

"There's a bathroom in the bedroom. You must have been out like a light. Most normal people get up in the middle of the night to take a leak," I looked at him sideways. "I'm sorry, to use the bathroom. I meant to use the bathroom."

"I'm not most normal people."

"I'm not touching that one," he joked. "Eat before you take a shower. I'm going to go run a few errands, and I will be back a little later. You're more than welcomed to stay."

"I need to get home," I said. There was no way I was staying at his place, especially not unattended. It wasn't like I would be a snoop or anything, but some men leave things where you can find them in hopes that you'd be nosey.

"Renee, it's okay, really. Besides, you might as well get used to it." Cockiness had reared its ugly head yet again. All I knew was that Stuart sure was going through a lot of trouble to win me over, no matter what his intentions were. I went into the bedroom to shower and dress. Stuart made it a point to leave before I did.

I sat on the couch to put on my Filas' when the doorbell rang. I didn't know whether I should open it or not. Hell, he shouldn't have left me here by myself in the first place. I answered the door. It was the UPS man.

"Delivery for Ms. Renee Matthews." I was confused.

"That's me."

"Sign right here," the delivery driver said. I signed and took the package. When I opened it, I found the most beautiful black and violet roses I had ever seen. I was at a loss for words. Only one person knew I loved black roses and that was Charlie. Stuart had mentioned during dinner that he knew more about me than I thought he did. That would explain why I haven't heard a word from Charlie.

I jumped in my car and headed home. I dialed Charlie's office.

"Dow Industrial's are down forty-five and an eighth, Chuck speaking, how can I help you?"

"Why are you avoiding me?" I started right in.

"Luv," he chuckled. "Long time no hear. How have you been?"

"Answer my question Charles Victor Thatcher," I demanded.

"I was giving you some space. I didn't want to confuse you more than you already were. So how are things going?"

"Fine, I can't wait to get back to work, I know that much." I knew he meant Stuart, but I used my better judgment and changed the subject.

"A few more days Luv. A few more days." There was so much I wanted to tell Charlie, but I didn't want to run the risk of hurting him. I wanted to tell him so bad that I thought I was falling in love with Stuart. He must have read my mind because he beat me to the punch.

"So how's Stu?" he tried again.

"Stu?" I said dumfounded.

"Stuart. How is Stuart?"

"Why would you ask me?" I was hoping that he'd admit that he was up to something. "Is there something I should know?"

"Only that I want you to be happy?"

"And what about you Charlie? Are you happy?"

"I'm happy when you're happy Luv, don't you see that?" My alter ego advised me to keep my mouth shut, but I had always been honest with Charlie. That was the basis of our foundation.

"It's your fault I'm falling for him," I finally said breaking a few moments of silence.

"I know, but he's good for you," Charlie said admitting what I had already known.

"What makes him any better for me than you?"

"Only you can answer that question Ree." I knew what Charlie was talking about; the racial issue.

"One day Charlie, one day."

"Ree?"

"Yes Charlie."

"Do me a favor."

"What's that?"

"Let him in. I know he can love you and I know he can do a good job. He's a good man. He sings nothing but praises for you."

"Charlie I don't want to lose you," I said; fear embellishing my speech.

"Luv, you'll never lose me. I'm not going anywhere. You and I are stuck together like super glue. But I know one damn thing, if he hurts you, he'll have me to answer to."

"That's what I'm afraid of; getting hurt."

"You'll never know unless you try Ree. You can't keep living your life in fear."

"Easy for you to say," I mumbled.

"Yes it is. You forget that I had just told you I loved you and wanted to spend the rest of my life with you, and you rejected me. That took a lot for me to get over. Part of me still hasn't gotten over it. I don't think I ever will. But just to know that you will always be in my life in some shape, form or fashion, is enough to help me get through."

I was in tears because I was in love with Stuart and scared to show it and also because I loved Charlie and in no way wanted to hurt him.

"Luv, tell him how you feel. Honesty is the best policy. Trust me on this."

Something was nagging at me. I knew that Charlie had my best interest at heart and I truly believed that Charlie wouldn't discuss anything of a personal nature about me to anyone else. But if he had been talking to Stuart about his obvious approval, I had to wonder what else they talked about.

"Charlie?"

"Mhmm?"

"Did you tell.." I paused for a moment.

"Did I tell who what?"

"Did you tell Stuart about us?"

"What exactly are you asking me Luv?"

"You know," I felt silly even asking him, but I had to know.

"No. I don't."

"Did you tell Stuart that we've been intimate? I mean you and I? Did you tell him about us? About Denver?"

"I can't believe that you felt the need to ask me that question. What do you think?"

"I don't think so, but I had to ask."

"Wow," was all he said.

"I'm sorry," I said. Silence. The silence went on for a few more minutes.

"Charlie?" I finally said. Silence. "Why do you continue to befriend me?" Even more silence. I knew I had hurt him again. I knew one thing, if someone hurt me as much as I had hurt Charlie, I wouldn't stay around. Tears began flowing from my eyes.

"I'll talk to you later," I said, after he still didn't say anything. All I heard was *click*.

After Charlie hung up, I sat in the car in my driveway for a moment crying some more. I finally pulled myself together and went inside. For the rest of the day I piddled around in my office thinking about Stuart; and Charlie.

Chapter 11

*M*onday morning I walked into my brand new office on Rio San Diego Drive with briefcase and my box of personal belongings in tow.

"Ah Ms. Matthews, welcome to San Diego." That was Pearl, my new secretary.

"You must be Pearl." I said in excitement.

"Yes ma'am."

"Nice to meet you Pearl," I said extending my free hand to her.

"Likewise Ms. Matthews," she said taking my box from my hand.

"Please, call me Renee."

"Renee it is. But don't be upset if I slip and call you Ms. Matthews."

"I won't," I assured her. I followed Pearl back to my office. It was unbelievable. I had a corner office with a view of the harbor. It was breathtaking. I pressed the speaker button on my telephone and proceeded to dial Charlie's number when he walked in the door.

"Charlie!" I shouted in excitement, nearly running into his lap.

"Luv!" he extended the same excitement and kissed me on my cheek.

"Ahhhh Pearl, what did I tell you?"

"She's absolutely amazing," Pearl said. I figured it had to be an inside joke.

I grabbed his hand and led him to the window. "Isn't this awesome? Look at the harbor and the boats. Do people really live on those?"

"They sure do," Charlie affirmed. I turned around just as Stuart knocked on my door. Talk about an awkward moment. My comfort level went from one hundred to zero.

"Stuart," I said sounding surprised and acknowledging his presence.

"Hello sweetie," he said, kissing me on the cheek and handing me a green plant for my office. It made me uncomfortable because I know it made Charlie uncomfortable. And I knew Charlie's presence made Stuart uncomfortable.

"Ah, the best man has arrived," Charlie said shaking Stuart's hand then extending him a hug. "I'll leave you two alone. Ree, I'll be back later." Charlie kissed me on the forehead.

"You don't have to leave Charlie," I said begging him to stay.

"Yes, I have to make sure that you have all the resources you need to transition smoothly." He turned to Stuart. "Are we still on for a game of golf later right?"

"I'll be there," Stuart confirmed. With that Charlie disappeared onto the other side of the door. I stared at Stuart wondering what that was all about.

"So does *your* office look like this?" I teased Stuart.

"Not as good, but I do have pretty much the same view."

"Where is your office?"

"On the fourth floor." My office was on the sixth floor.

"So how long have you and Charlie been playing golf," I asked curiously.

"A while now. He comes down from time to time or when I'm in Frisco we putt."

"I hadn't realized you guys were so close."

"Conflict of interest?" he asked reading my mind.

"Something like that."

"You love him?" Stuart asked.

"Something like that," I came again.

"Do you love me?" he asked.

"Something like.." I caught myself. "I don't know. Maybe," I said standing in front of Stuart looking at his beautiful brown eyes. "Maybe." I walked back around to my desk and sat down looking up at Stuart. "It's one of those things that we are going to have to see."

"Come to church with me this weekend," Stuart extended. God knows I needed to get back into church. I felt something was missing and I knew that was it.

"Sounds like a plan," I accepted. Stuart returned to his office and I continued getting settled in. I spent the remainder of the morning setting up my email, my software and my entire office.

"Pearl," I said over the speakerphone.

"Yes Ms. Matthews? I mean Yes Renee"

"That's better," I chuckled. "Do I have anything on my schedule for the next week?"

"C.S. will be in the office on Thursday at 10:00 a.m. The network administrators will be in your office this afternoon from two to three. Let's see. The quarterly forecast is due by next Monday. Besides that I don't show anything on your calendar unless you have something to add."

"Yes. I want to have a department meeting tomorrow at 9:00 a.m."

"I've got it. How much time would you like me to block out?"

"About two hours."

"So I'll block out nine to eleven."

"Thanks Pearl and can you send a memo out this afternoon informing everyone to attend with their thinking caps on?"

"Will do." Pearl was extremely older than Joanna, my secretary in Denver. I would have put Pearl at an easy fifty-eight. She was short and ample with red hair and matching glasses. Her skin was a pale white covered with tiny brown freckles.

††††††

Moving from Denver to San Diego had put me into severe culture shock. Denver was a segregated city and San Diego was a melting pot of sorts. It was a place where African Americans, Asian, Whites, Hispanics and others could live in the same neighborhoods; together. I found this to be true in both the upper middle class and lower middle class communities. I think I can get used to this.

I spent the rest of the afternoon preparing an agenda for the next days meeting. I wanted to make sure I had everything in order and was prepared for my new co-workers and most importantly that they were prepared for me.

"It's your first day and here you are, working yourself like a dog," Charlie said peeking his head into my office. "I love what you've done to the place," he joked. "You don't mess around do you Luv?"

"Nope," I said standing to give him a hug.

"I leave first thing in the morning headed back to Cisco. I wanted to take you to dinner this evening. And don't worry I've already cleared it with Stuart."

"Funny how you and Stuart go about planning my time," I snapped.

"Fiesty. Grrrrr," he teased. It was kind of funny because Stuart always said the same thing. The similarity between the two was uncanny and becoming quite eerie. I logged off my computer and turned off the lights in my office.

"So where are you taking me?" I asked Charlie once in the parking garage.

"There is a nice restaurant in Cardiff that I think you'll like. They serve seafood amongst other things. And we can sit by the ocean, watch the waves dance on the rocks and maybe even catch a whale or two." He had to be kidding.

We drove down 163 and merged onto Interstate 5. It was a nice ride, even with the over abundance of traffic.

We arrived at the Beach House Restaurant about thirty minutes later. I was pleased with Charlie's choice. The waiter escorted us to a table out on the deck. The ocean was so close I could nearly reach out and touch it. It was a beautiful sight to see.

"Charlie? What was that?" I knew I wasn't going crazy. I saw something out the corner of my eye.

"What was what Luv?"

"I saw something jump out of the water. It was really big."

"Probably a whale or a shark," he said.

"A shark?"

"Yes. There goes another one," he said pointing to the ocean. I saw it that time. I was amazed. "Do you see the little house boats out there in the middle of the water? Those are crab catchers. The fishermen go out to sea at sunrise and head back shore at sun down." I was really interested. Again, Charlie exposed me to something new.

"Absolutely beautiful," I said under my breath. The serenity of the water took me to another place; a place of peace. I moved my attention away from the water long enough to catch Charlie staring at me.

"What?" I asked. The look on his face made me wonder if I had a hair out of place or even better, a booger in my nose. He didn't answer me and continued to gaze at me in all seriousness. In my mind, I couldn't help but wonder if he was thinking about me with Stuart. I began to feel guilty and diverted my attention back to the water

"What's on your mind Charlie?" I asked as I watched a group of seagulls that had congregated on the edge of the water.

"Do you need any help out at the house?"

"Not that I can think of off hand. My bedroom suite finally arrived and Office Depot installed my office last week."

"So I hear."

"You sure have been hearing a lot lately. Ironically, so has Stuart." Charlie knew he did not want to go there with me. He was the one that told me to go for it. He was the one who said he wanted to see me happy with Stuart. If he didn't mean it, he should have never said it.

"Well if you need anything, you let either myself or Stuart know. We don't want you doing *anything*," Charlie said.

"And you know better," I reminded him.

"I know and that's part of the problem. If a man wants to do for you, let him. You deserve it."

"That's not the point."

"Women have taken this whole women's liberation mumbo jumbo too far. A man is no longer in a position to treat you the way God intended it." I didn't know exactly what it was that was bothering him. But whatever it was, it was starting to irritate the hell out of me as well.

"I don't know about all of that. I sure wasn't one of the many women burning bras in the seventies. Victoria's Secret cost too much as it is. I'm not about to burn what I paid good money for just make a point."

"You know what I meant silly."

"I know," I chuckled. I was hoping Charlie would laugh and rid himself of the cloud that hung over his head. And I certainly hoped that he wouldn't bring up Stuart. Much to my relief, he didn't. We enjoyed each other's company until we decided to head back to my place.

†††††

"You wanna watch a movie?" I asked Charlie.
"Sure."

"What are you in the mood for?" Charlie browsed my immaculate video collection.

"This one," he said.

"Bridget Jones Diary?" I exclaimed. "You can't be serious."

"Why not?"

"Okay. Note to self. Remember that Charlie is of the Caucasian persuasion."

"You bought the darn movie. So who's the real Caucasian here?"

"Ha, Ha. Very funny," I said.

"How about this one?" He held up *When A Man Loves A Woman*.

"Andy Garcia. Ohh la la. Good choice."

"I can run a ring around Andy any day," Charlie said. "What an ego." We both laughed.

Charlie and I talked for a few hours until we both fell sleep on the couch in front of the television. When I finally woke up, the digital display on the DVD player read 12:25 a.m. For a moment I thought that it needed to be reset until I looked at the grandfather clock that was displayed in the corner; it was 11:55. Yes I am one of those that set the clocks in their homes ahead of time. There is actually some truth to 'CP Time'.

"Charlie, get in the bed sweetheart," I whispered to him as I shook his torso; half of which was lying in my lap. Charlie yawned and stretched.

"What time is it Luv?" he asked.

"It's just about midnight," I told him turning off the television. Charlie retreated to the bedroom as I put our wine glasses and the open bag of chips in the kitchen. When I got the bedroom, Charlie had returned to *Sleepville*. I joined him.

††††††

I dropped Charlie off at the airport at seven o'clock the next morning on my way to work. Charlie's plane left Lindberg Field at eight-forty and I had to be in the office for my nine-o'clock meeting.

"Good morning Renee."

"Good morning Pearl. How are you this morning?"

"Great," she responded. Her smile was as wide as the Sahara. It was if she knew some little secret that she was dying to tell me.

"Any messages?"

"Two. Stuart and Charlie. Those guys are really crazy about you. I can't even get *one* man to fight over me, let alone two."

"They're just close friends of mine," I smiled at Pearl.

"Well one of them must think of you more than just a close friend," Pearl said handing me a bouquet of rose. "These came for you." Pearl looked over her red glasses at me. "You're a stubborn one, you are."

"Excuse me?" I asked her.

"Look, let me give you some motherly advice; not that you asked for it. Hell, no one *ever* asks for it." Pearl had her hands on her hips and a look of sincerity on her face. "You two are good for each other. Playing hard to get will only getcha' so far." I had no idea if she meant Charlie or if she meant Stuart.

"I'm not playing hard to get," I said covering my chest. I guestimated that Pearl was trying to read me from day one. The sad part was she was right. But I refused to let her know that. This wasn't exactly the conversation I wanted to be having with her, at least not now.

"Okay, *'Miss Not Playing Hard To Get'*. We'll see."

I chuckled at Pearl and walked into my office. If Pearl had been observing me so closely, who else had been observing me? I wanted to keep a strictly business rapport with my co-workers.

I prepared my agenda for the meeting and headed to the conference room. When I arrived there was one person sitting at the long, oblong, cherry wood table. She stood up when she felt my presence.

"Hello Ms. Matthews, I'm Angie. I am one of the research analysts in this department. Welcome to San Diego," she said extending her hand.

"Thank you Angie. Please, call me Renee. I look forward to working with all of you."

Pearl had made sure there was plenty of coffee and donuts. I placed an agenda in each of the empty seats and handed one to Angie.

"Look it over and by all means if you think I missed something or have any feedback let me know. Our goal is to get our numbers up and regain our title as the number one discount brokerage firm of choice."

I waited for everyone to arrive. One by one they trickled in. By nine o'clock, all twenty workers from my division were seated in the conference room.

"Good morning everyone," I said. Thankfully I was not as nervous as I thought I would be. "Before we get started, there are donuts and coffee at the coffee bar. Help yourselves, then we will get started." Mostly everyone grabbed a donut and a cup of coffee.

"We like you already," Roger said. "Coffee and donuts; I can live like this everyday."

"I don't know about *everyday*, but we'll see," I said. "Okay, we're going to have a getting to know you session. In front of you, you will find a list of five questions. You're going to answer the questions as they pertain to you, and then I want you to put them in a pile in the middle of the table. You have five minutes to answer the questions." Everyone started writing, including myself.

When everyone was done the lists were placed in a pile in the middle of the conference room table.

"Okay, I'm going to pass the lists out. If you happen to get your own list, pass it to the person next to you. You should *not* have your own list."

I waited until everyone had a list in their hands. "Does anyone have their own list?" I asked looking around the room. Everyone looked around and shook their heads.

"Okay. We're going to start with Angie. Angie is going to read the name of the person that she received and then she is going to read the questions as well as the answers."

"I have Lisa Kowolski," Donna called out. What is your hometown? Idaho. Tell us briefly about your family. I have been married to Dean for twenty-five years. I have two children. Rhonda fifteen and Avery twenty-two. What are your hobbies? I love to needlepoint, play golf and shop. How long have you been with Schwab? About six years now. What is your recipe for success? God, planning, God, organization, God, support, God, empathy, God, teamwork, God, ambition, God. And did I mention God."

I clapped my hands. "Very good. Lisa, it's nice to meet you," I said shaking her hand. We went around the entire table until we got to Roger

"I have boss lady's," he smirked. "What is your hometown? Denver. Tell us briefly about your family. I'm single, with no children and my mother lives back in Denver. What are your hobbies? I love to write and to read. I also love interior design and politics. How long have you been with Schwab? I have been working for C.S. about seven years now. What is your recipe for success? Hard work, teamwork, empathy, compassion, ambition, sacrifice, prayer, organization, communication, leadership and the drive to make more money."

They all clapped. "Welcome to San Diego Ms. Matthews," they all said in unison.

"If you guys don't stop calling me Ms. Matthews and call me Renee I'm going to dock each one of you an hour's pay."

"Renee it is," Dan spoke for the entire bunch. For the rest of the meeting I went over my expectations for the department and Charles Schwab's expectations for the company.

"I want you all to exercise my open door policy. We are a team, and it's going to take all of us to make this project a successful one." I adjourned the meeting and headed back to my office.

"He called," Pearl teased.

"Which one?" I joked. She sure is nosey, but I'm sure she means well.

"They both did, but you know which one I was talking about."

I smiled at her. "Nothing else?"

"Kent Colwell wants to see you in his office." I became nervous. Kent was the Chief Operating Officer of the San Diego office. I sure hope I hadn't done anything this quickly that would warrant a reprimand.

"Ahh Renee," Kent said when I knocked on his door. "Come in and have a seat." He stopped what he was doing, got up and closed the door behind me, then adjusted my seat under me.

"Welcome to San Diego. Charlie highly recommended you and has had nothing but good things to say about you and your work." My suspicion that Charlie had something to do with my move to San Diego was now confirmed.

"Charlie's an angel," I extended.

"Are you finding everything to your liking here in our fair city?"

"I am loving it," I said with glee.

"Good. Good. I received your analysis report this morning and I must say, I wasn't expecting something so soon. You are on top of things already and it's only your second day."

"I like to keep things in line if you know what I mean."

"I like that, and I am confident that you are going to fit right in around here. If you need anything, you just ask Pearl. She is your new assistant and if it can be gotten, she can get it."

"She's been such a great help already."

"Do you have any questions for me?" he asked.

"Not at this time, but if I do, I'll be sure to shoot you an e-mail." He laughed.

"Oh wait a minute. There is something that I wanted to ask you," I said.

"Darn," he said, listening attentively as if I was about to reveal who really shot J.R.

"Moody's rating for us last quarter was mixed."

"Yea," he sighed.

"Well I think we could have got an upgraded rating had we issued a statement stating that Joe Carellano was stepping down because he wanted to spend more time with his family as opposed to just saying he stepped down."

Kent raise his eyebrows in curiosity. "Go on," he said.

"Our stockholders are who?" I asked.

"Humor me," he answered.

"Our employees, their families and their friends. By giving a generic statement like the one we did last quarter, we left room for speculation. The rumor mills are spewing with talk of Joe stepping down because of wrongdoing within the company. It makes our employees nervous and it makes their family and friends nervous."

I really had his attention now. "They are left to hypothesize that something has gone wrong in the company and it is being kept hush-hush. Now, by issuing a statement that Joe was stepping down to spend more time with his family, it sends a message to our stockholders that we care about our families. After all, stockholders have families and they are saving for their families to pass on to their families."

"You're too damn smart for your own good," Kent said standing up and snapping his fingers. "Ms. Matthews, you have a long, promising future ahead of you." I cringed and gave him "the" look.

"I apologize," he chuckled. "Renee." I extended a smile and walked out of his office.

I walked by Pearl's desk and was greeted by the biggest grin I had ever seen Pearl possess. I smiled at her. "Anything?" She motioned towards my office. I saw Stuart sitting at my desk. I looked back at Pearl. "You're a devil, you know that?"

"I know," she said, fanning as if she were having hot flashes. I walked in my office and stopped in the doorway, staring at Stuart. The expression on his face was that of a child who had been caught with his hand in the cookie jar.

"Did I do something wrong?" he finally asked.

"No. I just like looking at you."

"Oh really now? And when did this happen?" he asked, apparently wanting his ego stroked.

"There you go minding grown folks business again," I said.

"You know, you try to act hard, but I bet that under all that tough exterior, there's a kitten waitin' to come out." I changed the subject, pushing him out of my chair.

"How did you know I loved black roses?"

"Because I know everything," he said sitting down opposite me.

"I'm serious," I threw a yellow sticky pad across my desk at him.

"Well," he said leaning forward and rubbing his hands together. "We were in the chat room a couple of years ago. It had to be right before Valentines Day because the conversation at that time was about the best and the lamest Valentine's Day gift ever received." Hmm. He had a good memory. We'd see just how good it was. He continued.

"And I remember 'Queentee1' saying that her husband had forgotten about her all together. And then you said your favorite flower was a black rose." I watched him as he explained using his hands and bodily gestures. Umph Umph Umph. Look at his big, dark, thick, long..... Whew! I tuned back into the conversation already in progress.

"I was paying attention to everything you said in there."

"Obviously you didn't catch the part about my dislike of arrogance."

"Baby, I'm not arrogant, just confident." I loved the way baby rolled off his tongue. Oops. There it goes again. Another hot flash. This man is proving to be a bigger challenge than I had originally thought.

"For a minute, I thought Charlie had told you."

"We *did* have *that* discussion," he confirmed. "But I already knew."

"I'm hungry," I said hinting to him.

"Where would you like me to take you?"

"Wherever you'd like to take me." Wrong choice of words. A sinister grin grew across Stuart's face as he put his head down on my desk.

"Let's go," he commanded. For once, he led and I followed.

I had my first fish taco. Since I had been here, everyone continuously ranted and raved about how good fish tacos were and cursed me for not having had tried them. They were good but they weren't all that. Hmm. Battered fish, coleslaw and mayonnaise in between a taco shell. Who would have thought?.

My cell phone rang. I looked at the caller ID. All the color nearly washed from my face.

"What's wrong baby?" Stuart asked.

"My mother," I sighed.

"Is that a good thing or a bad thing?" he asked. There were many parts of my life that I had not shared with to Stuart. My mother was one of them.

"It's certainly not a good thing." I didn't answer the phone. After it stopped ringing, I turned my phone off.

"You want to talk?" Stuart asked me.

"No," I sulked. My mother had managed to ruin my whole day. I don't know what I expected. Did I expect to never hear from her? I didn't know. I wondered what in the world it was that she wanted. It had been a few short months, and she's just now calling me. Of course, she wanted something.

Stuart took my hand in his and massaged it. I could tell by the look in his eye that he felt helpless. I took a drink of my Sierra Mist and took a deep breath.

"Mom; mother as she likes to be called. Well she and I have never gotten along," I began to explain.

"I guess that explains why you never really talked about her."

"Something like that," I said. I looked around the restaurant for the restrooms. "I'll be right back," I told him. I ventured to the ladies room and barricaded myself in one of the stalls. I had to keep my composure. There were some things I did not want to tell Stuart and some things I was not sure that I even wanted him to know.

I took a deep breath and checked the mirror to make sure that everything was still in its proper place.

"I don't know the real truth, but I've been piecing it together here and there. God knows I've heard so many versions of it, but Mama said my dad left after she asked him for money for an Easter basket. When he threw her a dollar, supposedly she poured hot grease on him." I tried to keep my composure.

"But then later I heard that my Mom was hoeing around on the military base in Colorado Springs and ended up pregnant, that I was the result of a one night stand. So truth be told, I don't know who my father is." I don't' know why I went through all of that with him. I suppose it was because I was starting to feel comfortable with Stuart.

"So anyway, Mom told me that I ruined her life. She said she was plain ignorant when she had me. And to this day she tells me that she should have aborted me when my grandmother told her to. My grandmother denies ever telling Mom that. As a matter of fact I think my grandmother knows the truth. She just doesn't want to tell me,"

I went on to tell Stuart how my mother tried to sabotage everything that I did and never wanted to see me succeed in anything I did.

"Why do you think she does what she does?" Stuart asked putting on his psychologist hat.

"Because she's a mean bitter woman," I gnarled. "Seriously, she always said she treated me that way because one, she felt if she hadn't had me, she could have made something out of her life. And two, she said she only repeated the way Memah treated her. Memah always said she was lying though. I don't know."

I looked at my watch. "Have we been here this long? I have to get back to the office. I have tons to do." I don't know how I let the time get away from me.

"Not to worry. I had Pearl clear your schedule," Stuart said in that annoying arrogant persona.

"You did what?" I yelled. I realized I had gathered the attention of everyone in the restaurant. "What gave you the right?" I asked in a lower tone.

"I wanted to spend time with you," Stuart said defensively.

"How about saying Renee, I want to spend some time with you, or Renee how about we go on a date or hang out. You don't change my work schedule. You're messing with my livelihood!"

Stuart looked at me in disbelief before he threw his napkin on the table and walked out of the restaurant leaving me sitting at the table. I watched through the window as Stuart walked out to the parking lot and kicked the tire on his car. He put his head down on the hood of the car. Perhaps I was a little too hard on him, but how dare he think he had it like that to go and change my schedule.

I walked out to the car and stood on the passenger side. Stuart just glared at me.

"Look, perhaps I was too hard on you, but you were wrong." Stuart slammed his fist down on the trunk of the car and paced around to my side of the car. If I didn't know any better, I just knew this man was about to beat my ass, but I stood my ground.

"Baby, why does everything have to be a struggle with you? Why won't you let me in? What is it about me that you don't like? Why do you keep pushing me away? I love you Renee, can't you see that?" A tear had escaped his eye. I felt like crap now. Stuart just didn't understand. He was making things difficult for me. The feelings. I didn't like it when men started to get too close. I don't know why. I couldn't believe what came out of my mouth next.

"If you want to stop seeing me I totally understand." I said it so nonchalantly that even my ego had to step back and say whoa.

"Get in the car Renee," Stuart demanded. Stuart drove me back to the office. The whole time he said nothing to me. The louder the silence got, the louder he turned up the radio. Toni Braxton was singing her unchanted melody of *Unbreak My Heart*. I caught a glimpse out of the corner of my eye and saw tears streaming down Stuarts face. I put my head in my hand and leaned it against the car window.

Stuart pulled up to the front of the Schwab building; I opened the door and got out. No I'll see you later. No goodbye. Nothing. He sped away. I didn't feel like working the rest of the day. I rode the elevator up to the sixth floor.

"What are you doing here?" Pearl asked me as soon as I stepped off the elevator.

"Don't worry, I'm going home." Pearl could tell I was upset. It was like she knew my every mood even before I knew them.

"That stubbornness isn't going to get you anywhere. Take it from me. You'll end up a fifty-eight year old receptionist at a brokerage firm."

I gave Pearl a fake smile. "Thanks for the words of wisdom Pearl. I'll see you tomorrow."

"If you've got any sense in the pretty little head of yours you won't be here tomorrow. You'll go and make up with that gentleman that who loves you to death. And it will be so good that neither of you will be in tomorrow."

"Pearl! I exclaimed blushing. I tugged at my collar.

"Well as you young folks say, Mama's just keepin' it real."

I laughed. "I'll see you tomorrow," I said firmly. Pearl just shook her head and shooed me toward the elevator.

On the way down to the parking garage my mind detoured back to Stuart. Stuart was a good man. I could never explain why I pushed men away. When I started to catch feelings for one, I sabotaged the relationship on purpose. There is nothing wrong with me except I don't want to get hurt. I will hurt you before you hurt me, was my motto.

"That's preposterous!" Charlie said when I got home and called him up.

"Charlie. I am not about to get hurt. I know he's perfectly capable of hurting me. And how do I know his intentions are sincere?"

"Well I'll tell you Luv, if I would have done as much as Stuart has to get you, which I have, I would be just as

pissed as he is. And I was plenty pissed, but I got over it."
I knew where Charlie was going with this. "How we soon
forget, how you hurt me. Now I'm not saying you did it on
purpose, but the truth is that you did. And I had to deal
with it. And if you told me today that you'd have me as
your husband, I'd jump at it. That's what love is Ree.
Love is the willingness to hurt for the sake of love itself."
Silence.

"I can imagine how Stuart feels now," he finally
said.

"What do you think I should do?" I asked Charlie.

"I think you should go over there and tell him that
you're scared. Open up to him. Tell him how you feel."

"I'd look like a fool to do that?"

"You're so concerned about what you'll look like
when that is not even the issue here. Renee?"

"Yes?"

"I want you to hang up this phone right now, and
go to him. And I don't want you to call me until you two
have made up."

"Don't you think that's kind of harsh Charlie?"

"Yes. I call it my rendition of tough love. Now go."
Before I could get a word out, Charlie had hung up the
phone.

This is silly I thought. Me going to a man. Never.
Never done it, never will. The little woman on my right
shoulder had appeared now. "You're the destroyer of your
own happiness," was all she said, and then she
disappeared.

I showered and threw on a long black Japanese
style kimono dress, sprayed a few drops of Organza,
added some lip-gloss and mascara and drove out to
Mission Valley. I knew I was taking a chance by going to
his house unannounced. He could be out, or worst of all
he could have company. What if he rejects me? I couldn't
take rejection.

I pulled up in front of Stuart's garage about a half hour later. It seemed that he was home; I could see lights in the house. I walked up the stairs to his front door and rang the bell. No answer. I rang it a second time. No answer. Oh this is stupid. Why am I here anyway?

I turned got halfway down the stairs when I heard the door open. I turned to look back. There stood Stuart in nothing but a towel from waist to knee.

"Please don't leave," he begged. I sized him up for a moment. Jesus get me out of here now. Make my feet run, far, far away. Please oh God. He held his hand out to me.

"Here is my heart. It's all yours. I give it to you for safekeeping. Can I at least see yours?" That was it. I was gone. I climbed the stairs and stood in front of him.

"I'm scared," I whispered.

"I am too," he whispered back. He took me in his arms and held me with such care, squeezing me firmly. He whispered in my ear. "I'm scared too, but I'm willing to take that chance." I melted like butter. The thong underwear that were dry just five minutes prior now were soaked.

Stuart kissed me passionately leaving me with no more self-control. He had me. He picked me up, still kissing me gently, took me into his townhouse and kicked the door shut. He lay me down on the covers that lay in front of the fireplace. I had to wonder of a quick second, why they were there. He looked at me with such passion and desire; the thought left my head as quickly as it had entered it. Much to my surprise, Stuart laid down behind me, spooning my backside.

"Can I just hold you?"

"Hold me," I said. He held me until I fell asleep. I didn't sleep too long. I woke up to Stuart still staring at me. He hadn't moved the entire time.

"I'm sorry," I said, apologizing for my earlier stint at the restaurant.

"Shhhh," he said putting his hands on my lips. "Renee, do you understand why I feel the way I do about you?" he asked. I truly hadn't the slightest idea.

"No," I said.

"Because since I was a little boy, I've had this idea stitched in my head of how I wanted my wife to be. I've observed you since the first day you walked into that chat room. Even though all the others cut up, acted crazy or just plain ignorant. You remained classy. You stood up for what you believed in and spoke your mind." He was getting mushy on me. I just listened.

"I remember sitting in on a conversation where the topic was about relationships. And you said that you believed that the man should be the head of the household according to the purpose of God. When those other women in there were saying they wouldn't let a man rule over them and all of that other silly stuff. You stood your ground. But you made it clear, that it would be the right man."

I continued gazing adoringly into Stuart's eyes. Over the years you still managed to keep your style and your grace. I watched you when you gave the presentation at the Techno Expo. Your poise was angelic. You represent everything there is about femininity. I knew at that moment that I was truly in love with you."

"I don't know what to say," I said to him. His dark eyes glistened in the firelight. I wanted to tell him how fine he was. That's what I wanted to say. But my better sense judged against it.

Stuart removed his arm from under me, laid me on my back and got on top of me, straddling my waist. I looked up at him. *God get me out of here* my insides cry. This fine chocolate brother sitting on top of me; I'm about to be in a world of trouble.

More shocking than Michael Jackson and Lisa Marie Presley's love child, Stuart pulled out a diamond ring in a black velvet box. "Just say you'll marry me," he said. My eyes got big and my heart began to race. I squirmed, my body letting him know that I wanted him off of me this instance. He obliged. I walked around the coffee table and sat on the couch. I put my head in my hands.

"Stuart what are you asking me?" I asked him as if I didn't hear the question.

"I'm asking you to be my wife. To let me be your husband. To be the head of your house and the protector of your heart. The way God planned it."

I didn't know a bout God right about now. But I was sure he had a sense of humor. Stuart kneeled down in front of me. "Renee I want to be that man that you wake up to, the man that you go to sleep with. The man you cry with, the man you laugh with. The man you trust, the man you make love to, the man you fuck."

Good Lord! Is it me or is it getting hot in here? I looked at him in surprise.

"That shouldn't surprise you," he said. "I want to build a life with you. I want to grow old with you. I want to take care of you when you're sick. I want you to complete me. They say behind every great man is a great woman. I want you right next to me. Do you hear me baby? Right next to me."

I don't know where in the hell they came from, but tears in thunderous burst flooded my eyes. Stuart held me, putting my head on his shoulder. "Baby I know. I know. I'm scared too. Let's be scared together. Let's become one. Be the air that I breathe." He took my hand from his shoulder and put it on his heart. His heart was beating so fast, one would have thought he had just run the New York Marathon. "Help me breath," he whispered. "Help me breath."

This time the constant puddle on my lap was filled with my tears as well as his. "You're the reason for your own unhappiness," I heard Pearl sing in my head."

I held Stuarts face in my hands. "Yes." Oh Lord!!!!! Where did that come from? I wanted to look around. Surely someone was imitating me. "Yes." I said it again.

"You've made me the happiest man on this earth," Stuart said. "Do you need some time to think about it?" Stuart wanted to make sure I wasn't saying yes because I felt pressured.

"You're the reason for your own unhappiness," Pearl's voice said again.

"Stuart, I'll be Mrs. Stuart Humphries." I said it with boldness that time. This time I was sure. I wanted to give this a try. I wanted this man to be my husband. I refused to fight it anymore.

Stuart smiled and said, "Yes!" as if his team had just made the winning touchdown. He hugged me for what seemed like hours. It felt so good to be in his arms. We sat on the couch cuddled up to each other the rest of the night talking about our hopes and our dreams and our future together as husband and wife.

Chapter 12

The months to follow, Stuart and I spent months getting to know each other and going out on dates. I was sure that once I accepted his proposal, the relationship would slow down. But much to my pleasure, they didn't. Stuart was more spontaneous, generous and affectionate than before. I had been going to church with him for two months now.

One Sunday as I was clapping my hands, getting my praise on to *Blessed in the City*, I kept my attention on the sixty-inch monitors that displayed the lyrics to the song. From time to time I would glance at Stuart who was in the choir stand. He was making his way down from the choir stand. Bishop Trotter had a big smile on his face. Stuart got down on both knees and buried his face in the floor. He broke out in prayer.

"You better come get this man. Because I know a few women up in this here church that want him if you don't," Bishop Trotter said.

"Amen," in various female voices rang out around the church. I exited my seat and joined Stuart at the pulpit.

"This man here," Bishop Trotter said placing his hand on Stuart's head. "Waited on God. He was patient. Most of yall in a hurry. Well I want you to see the results of waiting on the Lord." He waved his hand in my direction. "Stuart here has just announced his engagement to this lovely young lady." I was so embarrassed.

I was put on the spot. I hated being put on the spot. So what do I do when I'm put on the spot? I show out. I looked down at Stuart who was looking at me with a sense of longing and passion. I closed my eyes. This was all too overwhelming. An unexpected chill came over me and I turned to the congregation and blurted out, "Ain't he fine yall?"

Stuart rose from the floor and picked me up twirling me around the pulpit.

"Put me down," I said between my teeth. Stuart kept twirling me and smiling up at me as if I hadn't said a word.

"Thank you Lord, Thank you Lord," he began to leap in praise. "Hallelujah," he shouted. Bishop Trotter gave Stuart his microphone.

"Renee Matthews. God had blessed me by bringing you into my life. Because of you, I am a better man. I view things in a different light. Things that were once important to me are suddenly not as important anymore. The things I used to do; all of that has changed because God blessed me with you."

At this point tears had ruined my flawless make-up. I gave him the look. He knew that look meant he had better cut it short. He shook Bishop Trotter's hand then led me to my seat. After kissing me on the forehead he jogged back to the choir stand.

After church, Bishop and First Lady Trotter treated us to lunch at L'Escale to celebrate our engagement. First Lady Trotter looking good as always in her sliver and purple Tai Silk suit removed her hat.

"So what kind of wedding do you think you all will have?" she asked.

"On the beach at sunrise," I said.

"At church," Stuart said at the same time. We looked at each other in surprise. We definitely had to talk.

I had always dreamed of having a beach wedding as far back as I could remember. We would get married just as the sun was peeking out from the horizon. My groom and I would both be dressed in crème and barefoot. Our guest would be seated in white folding chairs in the sand right at the back of the ocean. They, too, would be barefoot. While reading our vows, the presiding minister would dunk my husband to be and I into the ocean, baptizing us into one. Our reception would be an early morning brunch. I made the mistake of sharing my dream with my mother.

"You're never going to get married," she would say. "You're too black, too skinny and too ugly." After that I don't believe that I had shared anything else of importance with her again.

"Just had thought that Bishop Trotter could marry us," Stuart said trying to get my approval.

"He can still marry us," I assured him.

"Sounds like you two have some planning to do," Bishop Trotter interjected. We sure did.

Once we arrived at the restaurant Bishop Trotter and Stuart dropped us off curbside and went to find a parking space in the parking garage.

"Marriage is hard work," First Lady Trotter said. "Marriage is hard work and the devil will test you every chance he gets. You must realize that everything is not going to be peaches and cream girl."

Somehow, I never thought First Lady Trout to be as personable as she was here. Even though she is petite and cute, I had always thought of First Lady Trotter as a siddity, holier than thou, thinks she is better than everyone because she was the First Lady, type of woman. I was finding that not to be the case. Stuart had told me that she made her own clothes. If she did, she did one hell of a job. I loved most of everything I've seen her in. And her hair was always laid.

"I realize that marriage is a partnership," I said.

"Yes but what you must also realize is that there will be times when you are in a partnership by yourself. During those times you need to stay on your knees praying. There is no way getting around it." I was kind of interested in what she was telling me. After all, she and Bishop had been married for over twenty years.

We spotted Stuart and Bishop Trotter walking towards us from a few yards away.

"Two things. Always remember. Once you are married, the marriage bed in undefiled. Make sure you keep him happy. Also remember that you are his backbone. Build him up, not tear him down. You will have better success if he knows he can trust and confide in you. A man wants to know they can run to their wife for shelter, comfort and protection. That is why a lot of us are losing our men, to women that will do what we won't do."

I let what she had said set in for a moment. Stuart and Bishop Trotter had reached us. Stuart's hand latched onto mine. After we had eaten and Bishop Trotter and First Lady had dropped us off at the church, Stuart and I had planned on going back to my place to celebrate, but instead we both settled on going to Best Buy to buy a few of the newest movie releases, going back to his place. We would eat popcorn and spend the time in each other's presence. We settled on Nutty Professor 2, Crouching Tiger; Hidden Dragon, Men of Honor, Romeo Must Die, Love and Basketball and Big Momma's House.

"Are you going to buy all of these?" I asked him.

"I sure am," he said smiling and shaking his head. "If you paid any attention, you would have noticed that I collect movies."

"I pay attention," I stated. "But now that you mention it, I didn't even see a television in your living room.

Stuart chuckled and shook his head. "You spent the whole night in the bedroom and you didn't notice the television?"

"No and I think I would have noticed something like that."

"I guess you aren't one of those women who look in people's medicine cabinets when you use their bathroom," he teased.
"No, because I'm afraid of what I might find."

"There is a thirty-two incher in the armoire on the wall as you go into the bathroom."

"Oh," was all I said. I should have known the cherry oak cabinet housed a television.

When we got back Stuart's house, he told me to make myself at home. I went into the kitchen and popped Stuart some Theatre butter popcorn and popped myself a bag of light popcorn.

The first movie we watched was Romeo Must Die.

"Aaliyah is a very beautiful girl," I said. Stuart didn't respond. I knew he was trying to play it safe. So I said, "don't you think so honey?"

"Honey?" he said. "That's a first."

"You like that huh??"

"I could definitely get used to it."

"Do you think she is beautiful?" I asked. He thought he had gotten of the hook.

"She's alright."

"She's more than alright. She is gorgeous." I tapped him on his shoulder. "You know I realize that you are a man, you are human and there are women you thought to be beautiful before I came along."

Stuart wiped his hand across his brow. "Whew," he said. "In that case, I think she is the bomb!"

"She is isn't' she?" We watched the movie, giving each other our own retrospect on the movie.

††††††

"You want to go for a walk?" Stuart asked me after the movie went off.

"Is it safe?" I asked.

"Sure it is." We ended up walking to a park near Stuart's home. It was beautiful. What impressed me the most about the park were the purple flowers that bloomed throughout the park. They were in patches and even two large trees centrally located in the park bore the beautiful bloom.

"So let's talk about this wedding," Stuart said once we were parked at a bench around a beautiful lake.

"Well, I had this vision for my wedding. I guess when I had the dream, I didn't think about my mates wedding wishes. I guess probably because I never thought it would happen."

"Why would you think it would never happen?"

"With my mother's history and my past. I never thought I would be getting married I mean I dreamed about it, but I really never thought it would happen." I began to feel like I was being dead weight. I had no intention of bringing dead weight into the relationship.

"What did you have in mind?" I asked him.

"Well I had thought we'd get married at the "Park" and have Bishop Trotter marry us." I could tell Stuart could sense my reluctance. "This is something that is going to affect both of us, and I want to make sure that we both are happy."

"I think this is going to be a little more difficult than I had thought."

"It won't be that difficult, because as long as I'm marrying you, I don't care where we do it. For all I care we can go to the courthouse and do it tomorrow."

"Speaking of which, we haven't picked a date yet." Stuart pulled me onto his lap, "When do you want to get married Nae?"

"Is three months a good time frame?" I asked him. He grumbled. "That's like torture."

"Well anything worth having is worth waiting for right?"

"Yes, he said. "But three months? Well if that's what you want, then I guess that's what you'll get."

"Okay you say now, I say three months. Let's compromise. How about a month and a half?"

"Can we pull off a wedding like the one you want in one and a half months?"

"Like I want? What are you saying?" I wanted clarification.

"You can have whatever you want just as long as Bishop Trotter can marry us. And ummm the water idea, I don't know about that." I thought for a minute. It was fair, actually it wasn't fair. Everything leaned towards what I wanted.

"Okay, you've got a deal," I said squeezing his hands. Stuart kissed me on the top of my head.

"I love you Renee."

"I love you too Mr. Humphries."

"I have an idea," I said.

"What's that?" he asked.

"Why don't we have our wedding on June seventeenth?"

"I know there has to be some significance there."

"Yes. It's six days after my birthday and six days before your birthday."

"Good idea," he agreed. After talking for a while, we had set a date. I agreed to get rid of the baptismal. Since I barely knew anyone in San Diego, most of the guest would be from Stuart's side of the guest list.

"How many people do you think you'll invite?" he asked me.

"I don't know," I said. I had to think for a moment. As much as I didn't want to, I knew I had to send my mother an invitation. I knew she wouldn't come, but I knew I would feel bad if I didn't at least invite her. I was definitely not inviting Marlene. After I thought about it, only about forty people came to mind, and most of them were from my old office and my new office. I didn't bother sending Memah an invitation. I knew she'd have some excuse regarding her health as to why she couldn't come. I didn't care whether anyone else knew or not.

"So you have forty and I have about a hundred," Stuart said. A hundred. Wow.

"So that's close to a hundred and fifty people."

"I guess I better liquidate some of my portfolio," I said.

"You will do no such thing," he said.

"Last time I checked, things like this cost money."

"Don't you worry your pretty little head about that."

I wanted to head back home. I had to get ready for my workday tomorrow. I wanted to soak in some hot sudsy water. My legs were aching from the new four-inch high heels that I had worn with my suit earlier.

"Do you mind if I crash in the guest room?"

"You know I don't mind." I left Stuart in the family room watching *Everybody Loves Raymond*. I heard him laughing occasionally from the bathroom. I ran a tub full of sudsy paradise, lit some candles, turned out all the lights and slid in. I smiled each time I heard Stuart burst out into laughter. His laugh was so joyous. I must have drifted off, because I jumped w hen I heard Stuart tap on the door.

"You alright in here?" he asked.

"Yes. I must have dozed off."

"Can I come in?" he asked.

"Sure." The steam from the water appeared to have taken away my energy. Stuart walked over to the tub and kneeled down.

"You're beautiful," he said. I smiled at him.

"Can I wash your hair," he asked.

"I dunno. My tracks are starting to get tangled."

"That's okay. I'll be careful. Maybe I can get the kinks out of your kitchen."

I laughed at him. Stuart combed my hair then washed it. He got a paper cup from the dispenser by the sink and poured warm water from the tub over my head. I leaned my head back, closed my eyes and let Stuart work his magic. He had strong, but caring hands. His hair massages could put me to sleep.

I felt a cool breeze, then warmness on my lips. Stuart was kissing me. I knew I was in trouble. Before I knew it, Stuart had jumped in the tub with me, clothes and all. His passion was unexplainable and overwhelming. My fight had been lost. I submitted. That night, Stuart and I made love for the first time. The next morning we agreed that the next time we made love it would be our wedding night.

Lord I wished these next forty-five days would fly by. I have to admit. One of my fears was that Stuart would get ghost, once I gave it up. But he didn't. He was more in love now than he was before we made love. I guess I have skills.

I left Stuart in the bed. I kissed him on his forehead and left for the office.

"I'll be in a little later," he said.

"Love you," I said.

"Love you too, baby."

††††††

"Hmmm. I see you, but I'm trying to wondering why in the world you're here," Pearl said when I got off the elevator.

"Because it is Monday and I do still work here."

"You also have a wedding to plan." I stopped in my tracks.

"How did you know?"

"Word travels fast around here doll. When something big happens at the "Park", everyone in San Diego knows. " I couldn't believe it. Word had got back before Stuart or I could tell anyone. I certainly didn't want Charlie finding out that way.

"Can you get Charlie on the phone for me?"

"Sure thing," Pearl said looking at me from over her eyeglasses.

"Hello Luv," I heard over the speakerphone when I walked to into my office.

"Hello Charlie. We need to talk."

"You're too late."

"Is anything sacred?" I asked.

"You have to realize that the "Park" is like E.F. Hutton."

"But you're all the way in San Francisco." I just couldn't believe that the word had gotten back to Charlie that quickly.

"I'm happy for you, and I'll be with you every step of the way."

"Charlie?"

"Yes Luv?"

"Thank you," I said.

"You don't have to thank me."

"No really. I thank you for everything. I thank you for being in my life, and I pray that you will never exit."

"Never," he assured me. "Now let's get busy. We have a wedding to plan."

Chapter 13

I turned onto my side and looked over at the clock on the night stand next to my bed. It was only 4:12 a.m. It seemed as if I woke up every hour on the hour. I had to get some sleep, or I would be a nervous wreck later on. I went downstairs and surveyed the kitchen. I retrieved a bottle of wine from the fridge, but thought against it. I knew if I drank it I would be late for my own wedding, and if I did make it on time I would be suffering from a massive headache. It was not the way I wanted to spend the most important day of my life.

I settled on a cup of hot chamomile tea instead. After I drank the tea, I decided that perhaps a hot shower would help speed up the process. I stood under the hot flow of water and let the soothing liquid cascade over my head onto my back. I didn't make a fuss about my hair since my beautician Shena was going to be doing it in about three hours anyway.

The nervousness seemed to worsen. Marriage was a big step. What if I failed? After all, let my mother tell it, failure was my destiny. This was one thing that I did not want to mess up. It wasn't like I had any good examples on how to create a successful marriage. My mother had never been married, and somehow that did not surprise me. If I were a man I wouldn't stick around long enough to be bitten by her bitter venom. I had read several books on how everything from how to love a black man to one hundred and one ways to please your man in bed. I must admit, I learned a lot; especial seventy-five more ways to please him in bed. But none of that really answered the questions that I had and besides two books I read by Dr. Ron Elmore, I felt the others were not tailored for African-American couples.

My thoughts drifted back to my mother. I couldn't put a finger on why she was so bitter. I never bothered to ask. I've often heard her respond, "Go to hell" when my aunts teased her about never being able to catch a man with the type of attitude she possessed. I really believe that something in her childhood hardened her heart until she got to the point that she forgot about loving someone else. But I have to say that I think she really and truly wanted to but just didn't know how. I was headed that way until I met Charlie.

I shook the notion of my feelings for Charlie. I had to keep those feelings buried; forever. Instead, I wondered what type of wife I would be to Stuart. I giggled when I pictured myself as June Cleaver. My insecurities had the butterflies in my stomach in full fiesta mode.

I knew how to cook, even though I didn't do it often. I had collected cookbooks over time, and every now and then would go into a cooking frenzy and try new recipes. Whenever there was a potluck at the office, someone would request one of my specialty dishes. Lasagna, shrimp fettuccini, sweet potato pie, banana pudding and gumbo were among some of my many specialties.

Every year for the holidays I would open shop, and take orders for cakes and pies. I would make a killing both financially and physically. Being that I am the world's biggest procrastinator I always waited until the night before the orders were due and stay home all day and up all night baking cakes, pies and other desserts. My feet and back would end up severely aching to the point that the next day I would deliver the desserts and come back home and sleep the remainder of the day.

Although I had watched every porno flick ever made, read almost every book ever written on sex and had a rather impressive "toy" collection, I still wasn't sure if I could continue to please Stuart sexually. I'm was a firm believer that *if you don't take care of home, someone else will*. I played our honeymoon night over and over in my head, but even I knew that sex is better when it is spontaneous.

††††††

I **must have** finally gotten to sleep because when the phone rang, the clock read 7:44. My hair appointment was at 7:30.

"Hello?"

"Girl where are you? You know I got out of bed this early just to do your hair. Now you know I wouldn't do this for anyone else." It was Shena.

"I'm sorry Shena. I couldn't sleep at all last night. I took a shower and drank some tea and finally got bed at five."

"Girl you that nervous?"

"Umhmm," I said, glad she understood.

"He's just a man."

"A man that I plan on spending the rest of my life with."

She grunted, "Ugh, don't remind me." We both chuckled. "Get your butt down here *now*. You'll be late for your wedding."

"On my way," I said and hung up the receiver. I jumped out of bed. Good thing I had taken a shower earlier. I threw on my Los Angeles Lakers running suit and some tennis shoes, pulled my hair back into a ponytail and headed to Shena's.

††††††

"*C*ome on and sit in this chair so I can doll you up girl," Shena said once I got to her shop.

"Now how do you want it?"

"I want a French roll but I want pin curls surrounding it," I told her.

"Are you going to be wearing a veil or a tiara?"

"No."

"Okay. Since you're not going to wear a veil or a tiara I think you would look beautiful with some light auburn streaks and some pearls placed strategically in your hair. What do you think?"

"I'm getting married, not trying out for the Miss America pageant."

"Girl this is your wedding day. *Your* day. You are a Queen. You're *supposed* to look like Miss America. It's not like you have to do much work to do so. You're a beautiful woman."

"I hope that Stuart will think so."

"Girl please, that man is so in love with you, he can't even think straight." I didn't feel so nervous after she said that. Women try so hard to please men, and forget that they *too* want to be pleased. What if Stuart didn't continue to please me?

I diminished the thought when I saw none other than Kevin get out of a blue Toyota 4Runner across the street. It couldn't be. Not here in San Diego. I must be tripping. The man that drove the truck stayed in his car for a few minutes.

"How much of my hair are you cutting off?" I asked Shena. I was still watching the man in the truck.

"Just an inch. You know better letting these ends get like this."

"I've been so busy lately, I haven't had time." The man in the truck across the street had gotten out and looked around before he looked down at a piece of paper he held in his hand. He looked straight ahead towards Shena's shop and started walking in our direction.

"What the hell?" I said out loud. It *was* him. What in the world was he doing here? How the hell did he find me? I never told him was that I was even moving to San Diego. The only way he could have known was my mother or Marlene. I prayed that he didn't see me. He was the last person I wanted to see on my wedding day. God was giving me a sign. I Just knew it. I had to call Stuart and call the wedding off.

"What's wrong girl? You look like you just saw a ghost," Shena said.

"I did," I said.

"Huh?"

"Nothing." I shook it off. I was overreacting. Kevin begin to change his direction and walked right past the shop.

"Whew! That was close," I mumbled. He walked backwards and looked into the window. *Shit.* He saw me. He entered the shop with a discontent look on his face.

"Renee?" he said in a high pitch voice. "Baby whatchu doin' hurr getting' all dawled up?" That damn accent. I cringed. He had come this far. He knew what I was doing here and I was sure he had come to stop me.

"What does it look like she's doing silly?" Shena butted in.

"I dunno. Look like she getting ready fuh a show or somethin'."

"I'm getting married today, Kevin. And why are you here? How did you know I was here?" I wanted to cut to the chase and send him on his merry little way.

"Married?" he gasped. "So yo' mama was right?" I should have known. For a moment he stood there and glared at me. Any look of glee had washed from his face and had been replaced with resentment and despise.

"Boy you're looking like you ain't feelin' well. You okay?" Shena finally asked.

"He'll be fine," I said. "Well Kevin I have to finish getting ready. Tell your mother I said hello," I said. I was hoping that he'd take a hint and beat it.

"You sho this is sumpthin' you wanna do? I mean you can't possibly be ova me yet. Right?" I looked at him. Now I know this fool had lost his mind. I didn't even respond.

"Right?" he repeated. I still didn't answer. "Renee," he was persistent.

"Kevin I was never under you to get over you. I knew after the first week or two that it wasn't going to work. No offense, but you didn't have what I was looking for."

"What was you lookin' for?" he asked. He tilted his head and looked into my eyes as if he was looking for the least bit of passion.

"Not you," I said.

"Renee stop lyin'. We are in love wit each otha." I was really starting to get pissed off.

"Kevin, when was the last time I talked to you?"

"Iss' been a while I guess. But I jes' thought you was needin' yo' space or sumpthin' you know how yall 90's wimmenz iz." I sat for a moment and stared at him. I really felt sorry for him. He didn't know any better.

"Do I need to call the police or something?" Shena finally asked breaking the silence.

"Naw, is jes....jes that...well...It's jes that I love you Nae."

I cringed and said, "Kevin if you love me, you will walk out that door right now and not turn back." He didn't move. He just sat there, staring straight through me. A tear tried to escape his eyes. He sniffed trying to hide it.

"Kevin, we are just two different people who want different things out of life. Neither of us are bad people. It's just that you want one thing and I want another."

"How you know what I want Nae? You ain't neva asked me."

"I just know it Kevin. Besides, I'm happy with Stuart."

"Stuart huh?" He stood up and walked over to me. Shena took a stance, with the flat iron in hand, preparing for whatever Kevin had in mind.

Kevin kissed me on the forehead, and took me by the chin and looked straight into my eyes. "I love you Nae. I'll always love you. You will always be my numba one gurl." With that Kevin disappeared from the shop. I had never seen Kevin so tender. I had to go to the bathroom to wash my face. Tears were streaming down in a steady flow. At that moment I felt bad and felt I was responsible for his pain.

Shena knocked on the door. "Girl it's almost 8:30, get your butt out here." I emerged from the restroom. Shena looked at my bloodshot eyes and said, "What was all that about?"

"Nothing," I lied.

"Well nothing looked like some unfinished business if you ask me."

"Just my past is all."

"Looks like you still got it for your past."

"I don't," I said frowning at her. "I dated Kevin a long time ago, and not for very long. After a month he was trying to get me into the family."

"A month? You mean he lasted a month? Girl now I *know* there was more between yall, 'cause none of your men last more than two weeks from whatchu told me. Well except Stuart. Oh and there was that white man. What was his name?

"Charlie," I reminded her.

"Yeah, Charlie." She put the finishing touches on my hair and turned me around to the mirror. "If you're going to get married, we better get a move on."

"It's beautiful," I said. he pin curls were jus the size I wanted and she didn't over do it with the pearls.

"You like?"

"Yes. I love it," I said checking out my do. "How much do I owe you?" I asked her.

"Consider it a wedding gift."

"I can't do that to you," I protested.

"I suggest you shut your mouth before I change my mind," she said.

"Yes Ma'am!" I saluted her.

"You still haven't heard from your mother yet have you?"

"No," I had tried to put my mother out of my head for a while. "I sent her an invitation. Oh well, I'm not going to let her ruin my day."

"Good. Now you get out of here and go do what you gotta do."

I thanked Shena again for doing my hair and told her she had better be at the wedding.

It was nine o'clock and I had to get my nails and toes done. I drove down Jamacha Road to the nail shop in Spring Valley.

"Renee," Lin said excitedly when she saw me. "Today the big a day eh?"

"Yes, so give me all you got."

"We a gonna make you look a very pretty," she said. Lin added a brow wax as a wedding gift. I gave her directions to the wedding and told her I would see her there. It was ten minutes until ten and I had to get out to the beach house in Coronado by ten to meet Charlie. The wedding was at noon, and I still had a few things I needed to do.

"Hello Luv," Charlie said as he opened the front door and kissed me on the cheek. "I had no idea you could look any more beautiful"

I blushed. "You're so silly," I said.

Various people were walking to and fro throughout the house preparing for my wedding. My wedding. That had a nice ring to it. Charlie had outdone himself. Fresh garland traced the spiral staircase, adorned with fresh cut white roses. A light studded, rose trimmed man-made walkway, trailed from the front door to the back door leading into the garden.

"Why are they decorating inside if the wedding is being held outside? I asked him.

"Nothing but the best for my doll," he said. He grabbed my hand, like a little child eager to shower his best buddy a new secret hiding place, "Let me show you the garden."

My breath was completely blown away. There were about twenty tables adorned with white table clothes, gold candelabras stacked with white candle and white roses, and some of the loveliest china I had ever seen. An artificial archway, also adorned with white roses and a sprinkle of black roses here and there, stood right on the beachfront in the sand.

"Where did you find black roses?" I asked. They were so hard to find.

"Who's your daddy?" he smiled.

"You are Charlie," I giggled.

I continued adoring the garden. A full orchestra sat behind the bar. Charlie had just gone all out. I started to feel bad that Charlie would do all this for me, and just months earlier I had declined his wedding proposal.

"I pray that he makes you happy, but if he doesn't, just remember that I will be right here," Charlie had whispered in my ear. Today would be the happiest day of my life and the worst.

"Renee!" I heard a voice screeching behind me. It was Marlene. I stopped in my tracks and didn't turn around. I had no idea how Marlene knew, because I hadn't sent her an invitation. Of course, my mother had gotten my invitation and told her, but didn't care to respond herself. I tuned around and tried to put on a fake smile.

"Marlene what are you doing here?" I tried to sound excited to see her.

"Is that how you greet our best friend? And why did I have to find out through your mother that you were getting married? You know this is cold! I suppose my invitation got lost in the mail."

"Today is not the day," I gleamed at her. "Today is not the day."

"I'm sorry. But you could have sent me an invitation."

"It's a long story," I told her.

"Well anyway, your mother is in the car," she said. I was sure at that very moment all of the color flushed out of my face. And that was very hard for a caramel complected woman such as myself. Charlie, who was directing the caterer to the garden, became distracted when I looked his way. His concern switched from the food to me.

"You did want her to come right? I mean you did send her an invitation," Marlene said. She was right. I did send her an invitation. I didn't think that she would come though. My reasoning for sending the invitation was to let my mother know that I was happy for once, in spite of how much she didn't want me to be.

"Ahh, and who is this lovely diva?" Charlie asked.

"Charlie this is Marlene. Marlene this Charlie," I introduced them.

"Ahh the lovely Marlene. Fancy to meet your acquaintance," Charlie told her in his usual natural charm.

"So you're Charlie?" Marlene asked inquisitively, looking Charlie down from head to toe.

"Why is she sitting in the car?" I asked sarcastically.

"She's not sure if she should come in."

"Well she is not going to ruin my wedding, that's for sure. And why would she come so far, just to act silly? You don't fly from Denver to California just to sit in the car."

"You guys need to talk," Marlene said.

"Not today," I said trying not to tear up again.

"Is everything alright here Luv?" Charlie asked me.

"I need to get ready for my wedding," I mumbled and walked up the staircase.

"Luv?" Charlie called to me.

"I turned around, "Yes?"

"Do you need me?"

"Yes," I told him and continued up the staircase. I could see Marlene's envy.

"It was a pleasure meeting you Marlene. Any friend of Renee's is a friend of mine. Make yourself comfortable and we're going to get this show on the road," I heard him say behind me. Ha. Some friend. The only time I heard from her was when she needed money. I hadn't heard from her since I had left Denver. I made sure everyone knew my forwarding info after I left. And today of all days, she decides to show up and with my mother in tow. I don't think so.

Charlie joined me in his master suite a few minutes later. He walked up behind me, and massaged my shoulders. Charlie always had a way to make me feel better. At one time I thought I was stupid for not accepting Charlie's marriage proposal. I had seen interracial couples and most of them went through unnecessary drama that I didn't want to deal with.

"You know that you can't let anyone upset you like this." I laid my head on Charlie's chest. "You don't have to go through with this if you don't want to," he said.

"I wouldn't dare back out now. You've spent so much money, and it wouldn't be right for me to back out now."

Charlie lifted my head from his shoulder and turned my face towards his.

"Listen. Do you remember what I told you that time when we were in the hotel, when you first got here?"

"Yes."

"What did I say?"

"You said that money meant nothing to you, and for me you'd give it all up."

"That's right. So don't think that you owe me anything. I also told you that night that I would always love you, and if anyone ever hurts you, they will have me to answer to." I looked at him with much vulnerability.

"I still mean that. If Stuart or anyone ever hurts you, they will have hell to pay."

"Charlie, what did I ever do to deserve you?" I asked him.

"I ask myself the same thing about you. And everyday that I spend time with you, I'm reminded."

"Thank you Charlie," I said smiling at him.

"Now hurry up, it's 11:30 and there are people outside waiting on you."

"Then hurry up and get out, so I can get ready," I teased. Charlie kissed me on the forehead and opened the door.

"Renee, girl you're messing around." It was Angie. "We need to get this show on the road. There are hundreds of people downstairs waiting on you."

"Stop lying girl," I said. "There is no way there are hundreds of people downstairs waiting for me."

"I know I saw at least a couple of hundred people down there. I even saw Tonex and Yvette."

"Did they bring the baby?" I asked.

"I didn't see a baby," she said. "I didn't even know you knew Tonex."

"Well I do and I don't," I began to explain. "I went to Truth Apostolic Church, and I met him through a friend of mine. His father and mother are the pastors."

"Oh so you went to the same church as he did?"

"Yes, and one day I just told him, that his radicism was welcomed and to shake the haters off."

She laughed, "He *is* different."

"Yes he is, but if you listened to his message, he is right on the point and tells the truth."

"There are some other folks down there too, but don't even ask me who they are," she said. We spent the next twenty minutes putting on my make-up and getting my dress on.

"Girl you are drop dead gorgeous!" She handed me a mirror. I looked at myself in awe. Vivica, Halle and Janet eat your hearts out I thought. Nervousness kicked into overdrive. I heard the band playing.

"Okay do you need anything before I go downstairs?" Angie asked.

"No you've done enough, and I thank you." I gave her a hug. "Can you please send Charlie up?" I asked her.

"Sure thing," she said and shut the door. I stood there for a moment and thought to myself, that not in a million years would I have thought I'd be standing here, preparing to become Mrs. Stuart Humphries. I had endured a lot during my time, and knew I deserved this moment. I knew I deserved a man that loved me, with everything he had. We would have children, and grow old together. I would the perfect wife he would be the perfect husband. Every day would be a brand new beginning in this new chapter in our lives. Charlie knocked on the door.

"Come in," I whispered.

"You ready love?" he asked peeking his head into the door. His mouth dropped wide open. "Wow!"

"Stoppit Charlie, I'm already a nervous wreck as it is."

"Wow!" he said again. "I'm contemplating on whether or not I should sneak you out, and fly you to a secluded island and marry you my damn self," he said. "I mean like, wow!"

"Thank you Charlie," I said hugging him.

"If he messes up once. Just once. Just an inkling," Charlie said. I knew he meant it. Sometimes I felt like Charlie was just waiting for me to come to my senses and marry him.

"We had better go, or else that is exactly what is going to happen."

Charlie helped me down the staircase and onto the rose lined runway. The band began to play "*Forever and Forever*" by Case. Butterflies by the millions took residence in my stomach.

Angie was right, there were hundreds of people. The ironic thing was I knew most of them. It looked like Charlie had pulled some more of his strings, and got everyone I knew in San Diego and Denver to come to the wedding. Some of my aunts, uncles and cousins were there.

As Charlie escorted me down the isle. Immediately I spotted my mother sitting in one of the back rows by the door. I smiled at her and became nauseous at the same time. She didn't return the gesture. I looked at Charlie, who smiled at me and stared straight ahead.

Stuart looked stunning in his tuxedo. It was cream and his vest matched the embroidery on my dress. He smiled at me. I smiled back.

"You look beautiful," he mouthed to me.

"Thank you," I mouthed back. He looked at Charlie, and Charlie mouthed something to him, but I couldn't make out what it was, but what ever it was Stuart understood it because he gave him the old thumbs up.

Once we had made our way to the beach and the minister, the music dimmed to a low tone.

"Who gives this woman to this man?" the minister asked.

"I do," Charlie said. He kissed my forehead and handed my right hand to Stuart. I smiled at him, and he winked back in observance taking his seat in the front row. I noticed my mother had replaced her seat with one up front opposite Charlie. I knew her intentions were to make me nervous, I turned towards Stuart, then towards the minister.

The ocean was a beautiful combination of indigo, royal and sky blue as the waves, rode to and fro from the sand.
The band had stopped playing. I looked in their direction and was pleasantly surprised to see Gerald Levert and Tonex walking towards me. I turned and threw the sauciest look at Charlie. I can't believe he had done this.

The band started playing, LTD's "*Will You Marry Me*". Charlie winked at me and blew me a kiss. Tonex was my favorite gospel singer next to Fred Hammond, and

Gerald Levert, good Lord! I had been in love with Gerald Levert since "Pop Goes My Mind".

Gerald began to wooo and cooo and my knees nearly buckled. "*Can't I marry him instead,*" I thought to myself. I was serious. I had told Stuart if I had ever met Gerald Levert, that I was history because I was leaving him for Gerald. I chuckled to myself as Stuart squeezed my hand.

After Gerald and Tonex finished singing our song, the minister continued.

"Hello, you and you and all the rest of you. Welcome. We are gathered here to share in the marriage of Renee Matthews and Stuart Humphries. Do you have a good prenuptial agreement?" he asked us. Everyone chuckled except for me.

"We don't need one," Stuart said looking at me seductively. "So uhh, can we get this show on the road?" Everyone laughed again. This time I joined in on the humor.

"I must talk about this thing called marriage. It's a partnership of two people. A married couple is ordered by God to love, communicate, honor, obey, submit, cherish, compromise and most importantly, build a relationship together with the Lord. They should not hide their feelings from each other, at the same time respecting the other."

I was ready to do all of that, so I had no idea I why I was nervous. I squeezed Stuart's hand, and realized that both our palms were drenched. He smiled at me.

"Stuart Humphries, will you take Renee Mathews to be your lawfully wedded wife, to love, to cherish, to have and to hold, for richer and for poorer, in sickness and health, in sadness and in joy, to share together as long as you both shall live?

"I do," Stuart said, looking at me with all sincerity.

"Renee, will you take Stuart to be your lawfully wedded husband, to love, to cherish, to have and to hold, for richer and for poorer, in sickness and health, in sadness and in joy, to share together as long as you both shall live?

"I do," I said with passion gleaming in my eye. I smiled at Stuart. At that moment no one else existed but the two of us.

"If there is anyone here today that does not think that this couple should be joined together in the Holy Communion of our Lord and Savior Jesus Christ?"

I stood facing Stuart looking lovingly into his eyes. Certainly no one would object. Stuart' s eyes were fixated on the audience. I fixated my eyes in the same direction as his. My mother had stood up. She was staring at Stuart with ultimate hatred in her eye. I looked back at Stuart and the same look had come across his face.

"What are you doing here," he asked my mother. I was totally confused.

"That's my mother," I told him.

"Your mother?" he said shocked.

"Yes. Stuart, what's going on?" Something just didn't seem right.

Stuart bent over to whisper in my ear. "I used to date her back in the late sixties."

I held my chest. Stuart and my mother had dated. I repeated it over in my head. I looked out at the audience at the hundreds of people that had come to see me, then back at my mother.

"Okay so you've come to tell me and the rest of the world that you've dated my soon to be husband? Is that what you've flown all the way from Denver to tell me?" If I ever hated my mother, I hated her at that very moment. How dare her fly thirteen hundred miles just to humiliate me.

"Why didn't you just abort me?" I asked her.

"I tried," she said. I wanted to take off my four-inch heels and beat her within one inch of her life.

"You're not ruining my wedding. I'm getting married whether you like it or not." At this point everyone in the audience were whispering amongst themselves. I looked over at Charlie as the tears welled up in my eyes. He stood there red as a beet not knowing what to do.

"You can't marry him, Nae," my mother said.

"Why can't I? Because you don't want me to be happy, because you were so miserable? You have controlled a lot of things in my life, but this won't be one of them."

"You can't marry...." My mother said before Stuart interrupted her.

"We can't get married Nae," he said. I looked at him and then decided that maybe I should beat him within an inch of his life.

"What?"

"He's your father," my mother blurted out. My surroundings seemed to revolve at an alarming pace. The only thing I could make out was the blur of Charlie running to my aide, before I blacked out.

Book Club Discussion Sheet

1. In the prologue, did you get a sense that Rosie knew all the times that she left Barbara Jean home on Sundays alone with Jessie Lee what was going on? If so, why do you think she continued to let it happen?
2. Do you think Dr. Reynolds knew Jessie Lee was the one that had raped and beaten Barbara Jean?
3. Why was Renee's outlook on life and herself so negative?
4. Why is that Renee shied away from love every time it came her way?
5. Why did Renee turn down Charlie's marriage proposal?
6. Why did Charlie continue to stay in Renee's life?
7. What was Renee's occupation?
8. Where did Renee meet Stuart?
9. Why did Renee continue to be Marlene's friend for as long as she did?
10. Why did Renee allow Barbara Jean to treat her the way she did for so long?
11. What do you think was Renee's reasoning for burying herself in her career?
12. Why did Barbara Jean despise Renee?
13. Why did Barbara Jean treat Eddie differently than Renee?
14. What did Barbara Jean do with the insurance policy that she had take out on Jessie Lee?
15. Why did Barbara Jean act like a victim when Jessie Lee died?
16. Why wouldn't Rosie take Renee in on a permanent basis, when Barbara Jean put her out?
17. Why did Renee remain close to Charlie?
18. Why was Renee so hard on Stuart?
19. Why did Renee dislike Derek?
20. Explain why you think Renee finally gave into Stuart?
21. Do you think Renee thought she would ever see Barbara Jean again?
22. Who did Renee refer to Gerald Levert as?
23. How did Renee originally meet Tonex and his family?
24. What do you think Barbara Jean's real intention was for showing up Renee's wedding?
25. Why do you think Stuart left Renee standing at the altar?

26. Most of you know there is a sequel to "Circumstances". What do you think will happen next?

Thank you for purchasing, reading and supporting Yolanda M. Johnson and her novel "Circumstances".